Deadly Innocent

Deadly Innocent

TRAGEDY ON THE TRAIL TO GOLD

Bill Gallaher

TouchWood Editions

TouchWood Editions Ltd., Victoria, BC, Canada
http://www.touchwoodeditions.com
This book is distributed by The Heritage Group, #108-17665 66A Avenue, Surrey,
BC, Canada, V3S 2A7.

Cover maps: Glenbow Archives NA-3351-1. Front-cover photos: Glenbow
Archives NA-483-3 (top right) and NA-949-80 (bottom). Back-cover photo:
University of Toronto Libraries P10092. Cover design: Ronan Lannuzel. Book
design and layout: Nancy St.Gelais.
This book is set in Adobe Garamond Pro.

TouchWood Editions acknowledges the financial support for its publishing
program from The Canada Council for the Arts, the Government of Canada
through the Book Publishing Industry Development Program (BPIDP) and the
Province of British Columbia through the British Columbia Arts Council.

Printed and bound in Canada by Friesens, Altona, Manitoba.

Library and Archives Canada Cataloguing in Publication

Gallaher, Bill
    Deadly innocent: tragedy on the trail to gold/Bill Gallaher.

    Includes bibliographical references.
    ISBN 1-894898-11-7

    1. Cariboo B.C.: Regional district — Gold discoveries — Fiction. I. Title.

PS8563.A424D43 2004   C813'.6   C2004-903544-4

BRITISH
COLUMBIA
ARTS COUNCIL
We acknowledge the support of the Province of British Columbia
through the British Columbia Arts Council

The Canada Council | Le Conseil des Arts
for the Arts | du Canada

CONTENTS

DEDICATION

For Ron and Barb, Phyllis, and the amazing Gallagher-Truter clan.

ACKNOWLEDGMENTS

My sincere thanks to: Vic Mazur of River Jetboat Safaris of Prince George, B.C., for a fabulous trip through the Giscome Rapids, and Brian Insko for the GPS information; the staff at Fort St. James National Historic Site of Canada for the use of their archives; the Hudson's Bay Archives; Lucy Larivière for the French translations; Marlyn Horsdal, for her diligent editorial work and patience; all the good folks at TouchWood Editions and Heritage House; Philip Teece for his invaluable encouragement; and Jaye for always being there.

PREFACE

The gold called and they came, from the eastern part of the continent and from California where the gold-bearing creeks had petered out. They came, too, from as far away as Europe, Asia, and Down Under, along paths that were familiar and well travelled. Some sailed the Pacific Ocean, others the Atlantic, around Cape Horn or on ships connected by a well-trampled trail across the Isthmus of Panama, arduous journeys all, during which the whims of the sea, malarial jungles, cholera-stricken towns and bandits imperilled their lives daily.

Still others came by a lesser-known route: a vague trail that snaked across the vast sweep of the Canadian prairies where the capricious weather sucked the desolate landscape dry one day and offered up floods of biblical proportions the next; a land gouged by myriad rivers and plagued by insects enough to drive both humans and animals insane. And that was the easy part. Beyond were the mountains: the Rockies, so enormous that they were visible more than a hundred miles away, and beyond them, a tapestry of ranges of rugged peaks and thickly forested hills that repeated itself for hundreds of miles before ending abruptly at the Pacific Ocean. Near the end of this vast mosaic was the place of their dreams, a place called "Cariboo," and only with great perseverance did hundreds of sturdy souls actually reach it.

Some did not.

PROLOGUE

CHRISTMAS DAY 1862

The snow fell in plump, soft flakes, piling up on the split-rail fence lining the pathway to the clapboard house and draping the trees in the yard. It settled on the gentle slope of the porch roof and, higher up, on the more steeply pitched main roof where smoke climbed lazily from a stone chimney. Webs of frost edged the windows through which the pale light of oil lamps gleamed in the early morning darkness.

She stoked the fire that she had been up twice during the night to feed, coaxing a burst of flames from it, and then added more wood from the box beside the stove. Now that she was up for good, she opened the damper a bit more. The seasoned wood caught fire quickly, sending forth a welcome wave of heat around her face. It made her think of her boys, so far away from hearth and home, and she whispered a small prayer that they were also warm and that no harm had come to them. The last she had heard from them was a letter from Fort Edmonton that had arrived in November. She had opened it with much trepidation, and felt weak with relief when she read that they were all fine. However, the date of the letter, August 29, meant that their journey was taking much longer than they had expected. Now, here it was

Christmas and she had heard nothing further. They had written of the mountains awaiting them, which had caused her much anxiety, and for many nights afterward she prayed that they had managed to pass through them safely. Surely, they would have by now. She thought about them constantly, her three sons, her flesh and blood, and lamented the unbridgeable chasm of months and miles they had left behind with their departure.

He lay there fully awake, listening to the strangled sounds of the river as the ice slowly choked the life out of it. God, how he hated this awful place, hated the cold and gnawing hunger. Even hated the men who slept beside him, one a next-to-useless invalid, the other so antagonistic. Were they asleep? Or were they awake, one of them silently plotting his demise? He would have to be vigilant just in case: stay awake, until he heard the telltale snoring. Then he would make his move.

Closing the stove door, she rubbed her hands together. A busy day loomed ahead. Company was coming for Christmas dinner: Her daughter-in-law, Mary, and grandson, Lucas, would be here, as well as Mrs. Wright, who was bringing her two daughters. Mrs. Helstone would be coming on her own, since her three children were grown up and gone and her husband was away west himself. She checked her image in a small mirror hanging on the wall and saw a rather severe-looking face staring back. Her looks had always disappointed her because she rarely felt severe inside. And lately, grey hair seemed to be sprouting like weeds.

It was a good idea to keep busy, and the Lord knew that she had more than enough to do since the boys had left. She would need to warm the house up by getting a good blaze going in the open-hearth fireplace at the far end of the kitchen. This would supplement the heat from the kitchen stove, which was inadequate by itself to heat the main floor, its primary use being for cooking and keeping the chill out of the house overnight. She went outside to the front porch and took a small armload of wood from the pile neatly stacked against the wall. It took four trips to fill up the hearth box, and she wished for a moment that the boys were here because one of them would have done it in two. Then she chastised herself for the thought. She was fully capable of making four trips: even more, if necessary.

A small rumbling in her belly demanded breakfast but she ignored it. She derived no satisfaction whatsoever from cooking for herself, so she usually nibbled in the kitchen now and then during the day. Nevertheless, tea was indispensable, and perhaps a slice of bread and preserves to see her through the morning, with all the work she had to do. She threw a couple of measures of leaves into a teapot and filled it from the kettle on the stove, then, at the counter, carved off a heel of bread with the new slicer William had bought her before he left. It was an unwieldy thing that worked a bit like a guillotine, and to tell the truth, she still preferred a sharp knife. A gift from a thoughtful son, though, did not deserve to be hidden away unused in a cupboard.

It would not be easy, this task he had set for himself, of that he was certain. But it was absolutely necessary, and of that he was even more certain. He reached down beside his right leg and touched the knife he had hidden there when he had come to bed. If he had done this once tonight, he had done it a dozen times, seeking, perhaps, the resurgence of confidence the weapon gave him. He gripped the handle. Even without removing it from its sheath, he could feel its deadly strength. It was a bowie, one of the finest knives ever made, and he was glad he hadn't scrimped and bought something cheaper and less reliable. The extra money it had cost would be well spent. It was definitely the right tool for the job he had in mind.

She toasted the bread on a wire rack on the stovetop, then poured a cup of tea. Not bothering to open the preserves, she dipped the toast in the tea, thinking how dull Christmas was without her family around to share it. Her boys were grown up now — Gilbert had a family of his own while Thomas and William had remained at home up until the time they all went west in search of gold — but it was the memories of when they were children that gave her the most pleasure. They would sit at this very table and thread garlands of popcorn and cranberries for the tree with a degree of patience uncharacteristic of young boys and, when that was done, she would have taffy for them to pull. She missed those days, when Christmas was rich with joyous things that filled a heart to overflowing. Where had they gone so quickly? Time was a curious thing, sometimes dragging itself across the hours while it stampeded down the years. Now, the big house was empty of everyone but herself. She could not even think about getting a tree, and other than attending church last night, the only homage she had paid to the season was making a large fruitcake and a plum pudding so that she would have something festive to offer visitors.

Dawn crept in the windows and brought her favourite time of day. Since she had been on her own she had found the pre-dawn hours the most challenging to face. That was when she felt the most vulnerable and unsure of her place in the world, when contrary thoughts crept like thieves into her mind to steal her optimism. But her strength always seemed to return with the morning light, just as flowers turn to the sun. After breakfast she cleaned up and then dressed warmly to go to market. The earlier she got there the better would be the selection of geese.

She had decided to cook a goose this year rather than a turkey, mostly because she did not feel that the bigger bird was necessary, given the small number of people coming for dinner. Furthermore, she had always maintained that goose meat was more succulent than turkey and lamented the fact that turkeys were supplanting geese as the main meat course for Christmas dinner. She sighed. The world was ever changing, sometimes not entirely to her liking.

It hadn't begun this way, and never in a million years could he have imagined this ending. Who could have? But things had just started to go wrong and could not be set right. There was no one to blame; it was just the way things were. Call it fate, if you will, for want of something better. They probably should have stayed at home, never come on this trip in the first place. It had seemed like such an easy thing to do back in the comfort of their homes, but the reality had proved to be vastly different. They were rank amateurs, city dwellers so far out of their element it was tragic. He wished he could go back to the beginning and withdraw from this adventure-turned-ordeal, wished he didn't have to do this. But it was too late.

Outside, the snow had abated and the clouds were drifting apart, showing patches of blue sky. It was cold, but there was little wind, so walking was quite agreeable. The snow crunched beneath her feet as she followed the road, a basket swinging from her arm, down to a narrow bridge spanning the River Thames. It had been a particularly cold winter thus far and children and adults were already skating on the frozen surface below. She stopped for a moment to watch and to listen to them. In a trice, her mind slipped back to the times when she had brought the boys here to skate away an entire morning or afternoon while their father busied himself at his shop. She had almost lost her Thomas here, when he fell through the ice, but William's quick thinking had saved him.

It seemed that with the boys gone, she was becoming quite an expert at recollecting the past. It was what sustained her and she spent a lot of time at it. Solitude breeds reminiscence, she thought, and few people would argue the point. She pushed away from the bridge railing and continued on her way, her thoughts slipping even further back in time.

She had come from England's London to this Canadian London as a frightened bride with a Scots husband who firmly believed that this was a land with a future. Despite her apprehension, there was at least some consolation in the familiarity of the name. What's more, there was also a River Thames, a St. Paul's Cathedral and, later on, a Covent Garden market. Naturally, all were pale imitations of the originals, but she found no small degree of comfort in their names.

There was, of course, no comparing the weather. The winters here could be dreadfully cruel and harsh, sometimes with more snow than she had ever thought possible, and the summers were often stiflingly hot with maddening swarms of insects. However, there was no denying that the air was much clearer, and the rich soil of the undulating landscape was every bit as fertile as the finest in England.

Her memories of when she and her husband arrived in town seemed to become clearer with each passing year. Yet she could not have forgotten the day if she tried, so bizarre were the events. They had come by stagecoach from Toronto in August 1830. It was one of those sweltering hot and humid days for which the country had ample reputation, and which had made the coach a purgatory on wheels. They could not pass through the town square, so plugged was it with people gathered there to witness London's first public hanging. Someone handed her a leaflet that contained "The Dying Confession of Cornelius Burleigh," the young man who was soon to be hanged. Apparently, he had killed a police constable.

Up on the scaffold, a clergyman offered a brief prayer for the murderer's soul, the trapdoor fell away, and he plummeted through like a dropped sack of onions. But the rope snapped as easily as string and the body thudded onto the ground. There was a huge gasp from the crowd as the condemned man got to his feet and stood there for a moment, swaying, stunned to find he was still alive. In an instant, the sheriff was at his side, escorting him back to the gallows. He uttered not a single word of complaint while he was fitted with a fresh rope, given another prayer, and hanged again, this time successfully. It was a ghastly scene to carry around in one's memory, but the thing that stuck in her mind most was how composed and serene Burleigh had been as he stared death in the face for the second time. Over the years, though, the hanging had taken on darkly humorous overtones as people referred to it as the town's only "double execution."

It was indeed an unforgettable introduction to her new hometown, yet so much of the countryside reminded her of England that it was not long before she grew to love it. As the years slid by, she came to love the town as well. She had watched it evolve from a small collection of wood buildings to a larger one of brick, and over the more-than-30 years she had been here, London had become a city. When the railway came in 1853, and turned the two-day trip to Toronto into one of hours, the city had grown phenomenally. It had survived floods, killing frosts and its own "Great Fire of London," and now presented an impressive skyline of three- and four-storey buildings and soaring steeples. The Prince of Wales had thought it important enough for him to visit in 1860, and it was then that people said London had finally come of age.

As the city burgeoned, she had added three fine sons to it and buried their father. He had been a shoemaker, with his own shop in Queens Street. The man had his share of faults, of course, the worst being that he was much too harsh with his sons and a little too quick with the back of his hand after he had had a drink or two, but he worked hard and provided well for his family and for that she was grateful. He had built their house beyond the flats west of the Thames, and while it was nothing fancy, it was roomy, sturdy and comfortable. When the boys became old enough, they took jobs in a tannery, but it was backbreaking work and they stank to high heaven when they got home. They managed to escape the drudgery by learning the shoemaker's trade from their father. William, the oldest, had taken over the shop when his father died, and the two younger boys, Gilbert and Thomas, found work in a new shoe factory. The factory was yet another sign of the changes creeping over the land.

My God! He had fallen asleep! For how long it was impossible to guess. His heart flopped around wildly in his chest, as if it had torn itself loose. It took the full measure of his will to calm himself and reduce the beating to a level where the organ felt anchored once more. He cursed himself for being a fool; it was bloody careless of him to sleep and he deemed himself lucky that he had not been killed. And why was the darkness impenetrable now? There had always been ambient light cast by the fire. Damn it to Hell! The fire had gone out! It was bound to happen sooner or later, but he had hoped it would last throughout this night when he needed its feeble light to carry out his task. Now he would have to wait until dawn. The endless night was trying his patience.

She was so lost in thought that she had almost reached the market before she was aware of it. The streets were busy with people and horse-drawn sleighs, a sure sign of the season as well as of the prosperity of the area. The War Between the States had not only increased demand for wheat, but also brought an influx of American families fleeing the conflict and single men avoiding conscription. The market, which operated daily, was more crowded than usual with sleighs and temporary awning-covered stalls in which vendors sold their merchandise. There was a festive air to the place as a choir of schoolchildren singing carols raised their voices above the general din. She pushed her way through the crowd until she reached the butcher's shop she preferred. A doorbell tinkled as she entered and she waited while the proprietor served two other customers.

"Good morning, Mrs. Rennie," the butcher said, when her turn came. He was a balding, smooth-skinned man whose broad smile lacked a lower left bicuspid. "Merry Christmas to you!"

"And to you, Mr. Beales!"

"And how are we coping without the boys around to help out?"

"Well, I won't speak for you, Mr. Beales," she said, smiling, "but I'm doing just fine, thank you."

Beales always used "we" in place of "you" or "I," which irritated her to no end. Usually she ignored it, but Beales was also the sort who thought most women were helpless without a man around and that irked her even more. Nobody could fault the quality of his meat, though, and that was why she patronized the shop.

She must be running a little late, she thought, because the selection of geese was not as good as she had hoped. Nevertheless, she found a bird that she felt would do, not as big as she would have liked, but then again there would be no grown male appetites to satisfy. She instructed Beales to have a boy deliver it, and left the butcher to other customers who had trickled in.

On her way back through the market she picked up some spices and a few other small items, then turned for home. Impulsively, she stopped in at Schneider's Emporium and bought three oranges. They were criminally expensive, but the Emporium was the only place in town that sold them, and it was Christmas, was it not? Sliced into quarters, they would make a delicious treat that might even surprise her guests.

A bit of a breeze had picked up and icily brushed her face. She pulled her scarf up until it covered her nose and walked as briskly as the snow would allow, humming the tune of one of the carols that had lodged in her head. Bells tinkled on a sleigh coming down the street and she waited for it to pass before crossing. She looked to see if she recognized the occupants but they were strangers. There was a time when she could not make this journey without running into someone she knew, but these days it happened less often.

The town was getting so big it fostered an anonymity that she did not much care for. Sometimes she felt like an outsider and she supposed that living on the opposite side of the river from most of the growth contributed to the problem.

The blackness was slowly changing to a dark grey as dawn crept into the shelter. His heart began to quicken again. It wouldn't be long now. The others were silent, which worried him somewhat because you could usually hear them breathe or snore when they were asleep. It was probably of little consequence, though. If they were awake when he made his move they probably wouldn't suspect anything and would think he was just getting up to relieve himself. Once up, however, he would have to move fast.

The lack of food had weakened him but as he reached for his knife he felt more alert than he had for some time. Suddenly, there was movement and a dark shape came hurtling out of the grey light at him.

She was on the bridge over the Thames when the strangest sensation flooded her body. Her knees suddenly felt wobbly and she thought she might collapse. She stumbled and the basket slid from her arm, spilling its contents in the snow. She grabbed hold of the bridge rail to steady herself. Her heart raced. Something odd had passed through her, something that for a moment was unidentifiable. It felt like another presence, at once strange, yet so familiar. An involuntary sob burst from her when she suddenly realized what it was. It had to do with one of her boys, and she knew with utter certainty that something awful had happened.

Part One

THE TRAIL

CHAPTER ONE

MAY 1862

William Rennie loved the smell of leather, loved its feel in his rough, strong hands as he worked with it, shaping it into shoes of all sizes for men, women and children. Unable to afford the sewing machines that were now available up in Toronto, he still stitched by hand. An awl, a scraper and a few other simple tools that he could carry in a small bag were all he needed to make a pair of fine shoes for even the most discriminating gentleman or lady, or a tough pair of work boots for a common labourer.

He took his work seriously, took his time, particularly during the lasting, or shaping, phase when he gave the leather the form that would determine its fit and comfort. Now, he took even greater care with the boots he was working on, because they were for his most exacting customer — himself — and they would have to carry him many a mile. Once he had the upper boot linings fashioned to his liking, he attached the insoles and the shankpieces that would give the boots strength, then added the trimmed, layered outer soles. Finally, he attached the heel bases and glued and nailed the heels to them. He removed his old shoes. They had seen better days, but he was always too busy making footwear for others to have time for his own, just as a carpenter's house is usually the one in the neighbourhood needing the most work. He pulled the new boots on and paced around the shop. The mid-calf tops felt strange and the lower parts stiff, which was to be expected. They would need breaking in; otherwise, they were a perfect fit, the result of the great care he had taken in creating the lasts. He removed the boots, dressed them with a protective coating of wool wax and put them in a cotton bag to carry home. Later, when the glue was set, he would begin the breaking-in process.

He glanced around the shop. It was not much but it had served him well until recently. He had not acquired one of the machines that would speed up and increase a shoemaker's output, but others had and were producing less expensive shoes more quickly than he could. To add to his problems, most shoemakers, including himself, now preferred working with cow leather rather than the old cordwainer's material of pig- and goatskin, and the big factories bought hides from the tannery as fast as they could be dressed. It made them harder to get and more expensive, particularly for those buying in small lots.

Ironically, both of his younger brothers worked in East London in just such a factory. Owned by an energetic man named John Hewing, it would probably put shops like his out of business in the coming years. Fortunately, reports of gold were coming from a far-off place among the western mountains, called Cariboo. As his business was hurting, these reports were irresistible and had infected not only him, but also his brothers and two other Londoners as well. In fact, his brothers would have left some time ago had it not been for him. Thomas, the youngest, had accused him of dilly-dallying, but Will was not the kind to rush into anything without first giving it careful thought. He might still be thinking about it had his brothers not threatened to leave without him, so he had felt hurried when he leased the premises for a reasonable monthly sum of money to another shoemaker with the proviso that he would resume proprietorship if necessary. His brothers, meanwhile, resigned their jobs and they all would make final preparations tomorrow after attending church. They planned to be on a westbound train come Monday.

When he thought about it, his heart thudded wildly but to be truthful, he was ready for a change. Even though he liked his work and found comfort in familiar things, he sometimes felt adrift, bothered by a nagging thought that life could hold something better. The pressure from his brothers to act aside, the last thing he wanted was to be an old man on his deathbed lamenting his inaction in the face of opportunity. Shoemaking had limitations that a few hefty pokes of gold did not, and if he struck it rich, making the long trek overland to the far west might be well worth the risks involved. It might even improve his chances for matrimony.

He was 31 years old, still a bachelor — still living with his widowed mother — and women were not exactly lining up to marry him. Never mind his humble occupation; he knew that most women did not find him attractive. He considered his nose too big, his face too narrow and his ears too prominent. His brown hair was already thinning on top and his down-turned mouth gave him a permanent scowl that had nothing to do with the state of his heart. When he smiled, he managed to look both happy and annoyed at the same time, and others often did not know how to react to him.

He packed up his tools in a leather bag. He would take them along, just in case things did not work out as planned and he was desperate for money. There was always work for a good cobbler.

Grabbing the cotton bag containing his new boots, he took one last look around, enjoying the familiarity of the place, then stepped into the street, locked the shop for what he hoped was the final time, and traded the smell of leather and polish for one of hops from Labatt's Brewery just down the street. It reminded him that a pint of ale at Haystead's before going home would be a nice cap to the end of his shoemaking days in London.

Later, leaving the saloon to a chorus of good wishes, he felt somewhat lightheaded. With the encouragement of some of the locals, he had stayed for an extra pint and now had to concentrate in order to keep a straight line. He was a solid man of medium height, and he walked with a plodding, self-conscious gait, as though he were constantly under scrutiny. Impulsively, he went to the market, still crammed with people, wagons and horses, and bought his mother a gift, a formidable-looking bread slicer that he thought she would find convenient. Buying her gifts when she least expected them was something he did from time to time as it was the only way he knew to express his deep love for her. The proprietor put it in a wooden box and Will took his leave.

Thinking that a good walk would help clear his head, he decided to take the long way home, up to Blackfriars Bridge and across the Thames there. He turned onto Ridout Street and where the boardwalks ended, he passed between the towering beech trees that lined its upper reaches. It was as pretty a walk as you would find in a city anywhere, especially on a glorious spring evening. To his left he could see Eldon House, perched on the terraced slope well above the river among trees and shrubs cared for by gardeners, its elegant Victorian lines enhanced by flowered vines in full bloom. It was the home of John Harris, father of eight beautiful daughters, once the town's prize catches, all of whom were married now. But Eldon House was also the place where

London's elite met for their fancy soirées, and no place for a lowly cobbler. The thought ruffled him as he crossed the murky, languid river that moved as slowly to its end in Lake St. Clair as he himself moved through life. A few pokes of gold would go a long way toward widening the narrow perspectives held by a certain class of people in this town.

To the right was Kent Street, along which were the homes of the two men who would be joining Will and his brothers on the journey west. Gilbert and Thomas worked with one of the pair, but Will had met them for the first time only a couple of weeks ago. They seemed to be competent men, although John Helstone, whom Will guessed to be in his 50s, had a disagreeable air of self-righteousness about him. He was not the sort of person Will would have readily made friends with under normal circumstances, and Thomas's dislike for the man seemed to crystallize at their first meeting. But there was no denying that he could be entertaining at times. He had worked most of his adult life as a hospital orderly and told with great relish many gruesome and ribald tales about doctors and their mishaps. He also claimed that he had readily volunteered to fall in behind Colonel James Fitzgibbon on his march to Montgomery's tavern to put an end to William Lyon Mackenzie's notions about responsible government. "We rode up Yonge Street," he had said, "with flags flying from all the houses and the people cheering us on. I have never felt so proud. When we put a cannonball right through the tavern, the rebels scattered and went back into whatever hole they crawled out of." He boasted that being fired upon had thrilled him every bit as much as that decisive cannon blast. "It all ended too soon," he added with a smile devoid of warmth and friendliness.

So the man's a Tory, Will thought, and a dyed-in-the-wool one at that. As a Grit, he did not think that marching with Fitzgibbon was anything to brag about but refrained from commenting; it was no time to be declaring political loyalties.

Altogether, Helstone seemed an odd sort, more the stay-at-home-type content with the status quo, not the kind to be joining a risky expedition like this. Then there was his age. Curious, Will had asked him his reasons for going.

"This is the Age of Gold, my friend, and I want my share. It's as simple as that," Helstone had replied.

John Wright, the other man, was a fairly recent arrival from England and a nephew of Helstone's. Just 25 years old, he had a wife and two daughters to whom he too would bid farewell. Like the Rennies, he was a shoemaker and had worked alongside Will's brothers at the factory. He was a self-effacing, compliant sort and had allowed Helstone to persuade him to join the expedition; otherwise, he would have happily remained at home. When the Rennies brought talk of gold into the factory, it had not excited him all that much. He was quite satisfied with his job and deemed going to the goldfields and leaving a wife and two daughters behind, even if it was temporary, tantamount to deserting them. But he had made the mistake of telling his uncle that the Rennies were forming a party to go west. Helstone seized upon the idea and then convinced him that he should go too. "Look, Johnny," he had said, "if you're going to work like a slave you might as well do it for yourself rather than someone else." Wright agreed but was still disinclined to go, an awkward position when he typically deferred to dominant people like his uncle. Helstone, though, was a persuasive man and never let up, peeling away layer after layer of his nephew's resolve. Elizabeth, his wife, prevailed upon him to go to, saying, "It would be a good thing, John. You were a cordwainer in England and you are a cordwainer here. Is that what you want for the rest of your life? Besides, think of how you could provide for me and the girls."

Wright was still not convinced that it was a good idea, but the pressure on him was too great. He gave in.

They were all such different personalities that Will had no idea how they would get along, but he felt that greater numbers would only enhance safety and economy. Besides, the journey would be their common ground and that should serve as the glue to hold them together.

After the others had gone for help, he and his companions played parlour games to help pass the long hours. One of them would think of an object and the others would try to guess what it was. They were given no clues other than "large" or "small" and they could only ask questions that could be answered with "yes" or "no." The idea was not to guess the answer until you were reasonably sure what it was, otherwise the game would end and the person who "thought of something" would win. His companions made their objects easy but his were always difficult. He could tell that they resented it, but neither said anything.

They also played "The Minister's Cat," a game in which the cat was described by an adjective that began with the letter A. This went on around the circle until a person was unable to come up with an adjective and was out of the game. The remaining players would continue with the letter B. Since there were just three players, each game lasted for only two letters. However, over the days they had managed to work their way through the entire alphabet. He always won because he knew words of which the others had never heard. This was another cause of resentment but even that took their minds off the more serious problem: their survival.

There was work to do in the camp, mostly gathering wood and keeping the fire going. This was a monumental task, considering their condition, but movement was imperative for it warmed them and made them feel more alive. At first they kept a bonfire, albeit a smoky one, but soon they realized that they were going through the wood too fast and reduced the blaze to a more modest size.

All were still having problems with frozen hands and feet. They could not thaw them out slowly in warm water, the preferred method, as they had no receptacle large enough for the job, and thawing them out by placing them near the fire was not only awkward, it was horribly painful and raised ugly blisters. Nor did they have enough extra clothing or buffalo robes with which to wrap them at night, since they needed to wear what they had to keep the rest of their bodies from freezing. They coped, however, and even if they were nearly cripples, they had enough mobility to move around the general area of the camp. So far, no one was inclined to give up. Not yet anyway.

Will's mother was preparing dinner in the kitchen when he arrived home. He often felt a mild jolt when he saw her because of their similar facial features. Despite her perpetual frown, she was a warm, sincere person who loved her three sons unconditionally. Their father had died several years ago from a cancer and she doted on them unashamedly. She was devastated that they were all leaving at once, and they tried to comfort her, saying they would return with wealth that a king would envy. She would not be consoled though, and countered simply with, "You are my wealth and all that I need."

Few things escaped her eye, or her nose for that matter, and she complimented Will on his new boots when he showed them to her, adding, "It was wise of you to not to overstay your welcome at Haystead's."

He shook his head and laughed. "It's impossible to keep anything from you, Mother," he said, then added jokingly, "For 30 years you've kept me on the straight and narrow and in appreciation of your hard work and dedication, I've brought you a small gift." Knowing how easy it was to pique her curiosity, he placed the box on the counter and said, "But you can't open it until after I'm gone."

"You are the cruellest of all my sons," she said, smiling, and before she could add anything further, he was out the back door to the privy to rid himself of his liquid burden.

When he returned, Thomas had arrived home from work and was in the parlour reading the newspaper. Twenty-three years old, he had apprenticed with Will before taking a job in Hewing's factory, which he had cheerfully resigned in order to make the journey west for gold. Yet it was not the gold that attracted him as much as it was the adventure of looking for it and the opportunity to seek new horizons. He had been seriously courting a young lady — the daughter of a fellow factory worker — but when he broached the subject of marriage, the girl suddenly broke off the relationship, saying her father was a cobbler and she did not want to marry one. Thomas was hurt by the rejection, so the gold rush in British Columbia came along at exactly the right time. He was impatient for Monday and their departure.

Completely opposite to Will, who was as patient and methodical as their mother, Thomas took after their father, ardent and free-spirited, with the same intense, restless eyes, thick dark hair and thin, bearded face. Indeed, the two brothers hardly looked related at all, and it was not until they were with Gilbert, who shared traits from both parents, that the connection was apparent. As adults, their relationship could sometimes be stormy, but it was the thinnest of veneers beneath which lay a strong fondness for each other. After their father died, Thomas had often looked to Will for guidance, and the pair had formed an unbreakable bond. When Thomas had served his apprenticeship, the brothers seemed more like father and son, a feeling that Will had liked and even nurtured. But Thomas had grown into his own man, and though elements of his personality often clashed with Will's, it was those very elements that led Will to believe Thomas might one day rise above cobbling shoes for a living, and why he thought the call for gold rang so loudly in his brother's ears.

"We've made the newspaper, Will. It's only a few lines, but we are wished well and the hope is that we're not leaving too late in the season for an overland journey. Others, they say, left various parts of Canada nearly a month ago."

"How would they know it's late when they've never made the trip themselves? The information I've read says that it can be done in just a few short weeks, so I wouldn't worry if I were you. We have plenty of time."

"We will if the information we have is accurate. But what if it isn't? I think we ought to have left much earlier, just in case."

"Maybe so, but if we'd left earlier we wouldn't now be about to enjoy another of Mother's home-cooked meals. So stop complaining," he added good-naturedly. "Let's go eat!"

Thomas looked as if he was ready for a good argument, but backed off.

Despite the lightheartedness of his words, Will felt a pang of guilt. His procrastinations had indeed delayed them, but the decision to go west was so life-changing that he had needed time to think it through. Even so, he was reasonably certain that it would not take long to reach Cariboo. An advertisement placed in the local paper by the British Columbia Overland Transit Company, which Will presumed would know these things, estimated only 12 days from Lake Superior to the goldfields. He and his brothers would be leaving on May 15, so even allowing for delays, they ought to be able reach the mines by the end of June at the very latest. If the reports were as good as he had heard, that would still leave plenty of time to line their pockets with gold before winter was upon them.

The two men joined their mother for a hearty dinner of ham, along with turnips and potatoes that tasted of the storage they had been in over the winter. But summer was almost here and it wouldn't be long before plenty of fresh vegetables would be available from their own garden as well as from the farmers who sold their produce in Covent Garden. All through dinner, Will was aware of his mother staring at him and Thomas. He wondered if she were trying to fix their images in her mind so that she would never forget them. He knew that she would miss them terribly, and her gaze made him feel slightly uncomfortable and more than a little anxious. He and his brothers were pulling up stakes all at once and leaving her to fend for herself, on her own for the first time in her life. It was a worrisome prospect, and he hoped that she would be all right.

Afterward, Will went for a long walk to begin the process of breaking in his new boots. By the time he returned home, the little toes on both feet felt much abused, but the leather was definitely more pliable than it had been. He rubbed some oil into the toe areas of the boots, pleased with the progress.

He arose early the following morning and went for another long walk before attending church. The boots were just fine. Some of the congregation who knew him and his brothers wished them well on their journey while others clearly deemed them mad. Most of the latter, Will thought, were probably envious and secretly wished they had the wherewithal and courage to do the same thing. The minister, whom Will considered a tyrant, mentioned the brothers' pending journey and led a short prayer for their safety. Afterward he made a point of shaking their hands as they left. "God be with you," he said, and reminded them to not forget to observe the Sabbath nor to take along a Bible. "It won't replace a church, but having the word of God as near as your carpet bag should be most helpful."

Will felt some colour creep into his cheeks, for he had not opened his Bible since his early teens. Gilbert had not either, but Thomas had and would take his. It was a book his younger brother felt a need to read from time to time.

Will spent the afternoon in the parlour going over maps of the North-Western Territory and reading Francis Parkman's *The Oregon Trail*. The author's experiences travelling across the prairies and through the mountains were fascinating. Some of his encounters with Indians were downright alarming and caused Will not a little concern for his own safety: Indians were his greatest fear. As for the maps, well, they were probably highly inaccurate, but at least they gave him some sense of the land he would be crossing, which was vast by any standards. He hoped that better, more recent issues might be available at Fort Garry. He was still studying the maps when Gilbert arrived with his wife, Mary, and their toddler, Lucas, to enjoy a last family dinner together.

Two years Will's junior, Gilbert was the tallest of the three brothers, with a ruggedness to his looks that women found attractive and Will envied. Considered aloof by many who met him, he was a quiet man who saw life in absolutes: things were black or they were white, with no grey area in between. There was also a directness about him that sometimes put people on the defensive, particularly Will if he was feeling vulnerable. It was not anything that Gilbert did intentionally; it was just his style, nothing more. He could be imperturbable, too, except when he had to act as an intermediary between Thomas's impulsiveness and Will's caution. It was a role that he sometimes found exasperating, and he did not always bear it with good humour.

While the women cooked dinner and tended to Lucas, the brothers, now joined by Thomas, looked the maps and discussed strategy amidst much speculation about the challenge facing them. Like Will, both Gilbert and Thomas believed that Indians would be the biggest threat to their safety. The atmosphere was charged with the excitement that always precedes great adventures. Will and Thomas did their best to avoid the topic of their late departure for the mines, but eventually their good intentions slipped into bickering.

Gilbert held up his hands. "Enough, the both of you! You sound like the worst fishwives in the world. If you do this on the trip, I'll want at least a mile between us." It was not uncommon for Gilbert to put distance between himself and his brothers at the best of times, and Will believed it to be one of the main reasons why he was grateful to have found Mary and made a home of his own.

Will shrugged and put the bickering down to tension. It was the nature of most adventures to generate high spirits, and high spirits were usually a tightrope of emotions. They would be all right once they were underway and concentrating on the demands of the journey.

They enjoyed a sumptuous dinner of roast beef and vegetables garnished with tomato ketchup, followed by melon preserves for dessert. Acutely aware that a poverty of meals awaited him on the trail, Will relished his mother's cooking down to the last morsel. Afterward, while the women cleaned up the kitchen, the men adjourned to the parlour for a glass of port and a pipe. Upon finishing their chores, the women joined them. Mrs. Rennie, needing to keep her hands busy, worked on her *petit point*, a mallard on the wing that was near completion, and Mary sat curled up with Lucas on the settee. Like the adults, Lucas was subdued by an abundance of food. The level in the men's glasses fell rather quickly and Will refilled them while Gilbert and Thomas did their best to reassure their mother that they were embarking on a great adventure and not heading to their doom.

"I have spent sleepless nights debating that very point with myself," said Mrs. Rennie. "But worrying is a mother's prerogative and no mother would deserve the title if she did not." She looked at her daughter-in-law for a comment.

Mary sighed. "I try not to think of it," she said. "When I do, I worry far more than I should, which seems a waste of time. Better to think of gold and all the things one could do with it."

"That's the spirit," Thomas said, smiling. "This little jaunt will change our lives completely, I'm convinced of it." Only half-joking, he added, "They'll be begging for our company over at Eldon House, mark my words."

Mrs. Rennie asked to be reminded once again of the route they would take to Fort Garry.

"Our plan," said Will, "is to take the train to Detroit, Chicago, Milwaukee and La Crosse, on the Mississippi River. That's as far west as the train goes. From there we've booked passage on a steamer to St. Paul. After that, we'll have to play things by ear. I've been told that a stagecoach runs from St. Paul to Georgetown, which is even farther west, on the Red River of the North, and that a steamer runs regularly downriver to Fort Garry. It's as easy as that. I expect that the worst part of the trip will be the 300-mile stagecoach run from St. Paul to Georgetown. It's sure to give our bones a good rattling. At any rate, it shouldn't take more than 10 days or so to get to Fort Garry and a couple of weeks at most to get from there to the goldfields. That part probably won't be easy, but if it was, then everybody would be doing it. In any case, three to four weeks should see us there."

Thomas interjected, "It's also a whole lot more affordable than the Panama route."

This was important, because each brother was putting his life's savings into the adventure, anticipating that it would ultimately pay excellent dividends.

Talk of the trip was put aside when Mrs. Rennie asked Thomas to bring out the concertina and play a song. The instrument had once belonged to her husband who played it sporadically, usually when in his cups. Will had tried to play but had no facility for it, nor did Gilbert. Thomas not only had the desire to play it, but also possessed the ability; he was self-taught and quite good. He sang, too, with a not unpleasant voice and broke out into a spirited rendition of "The Rapids," a voyageur song he had learned at school: "Row brothers row, the stream runs fast/ The rapids are near and the daylight's past." He had the others join in on "Pop Goes the Weasel" and "Oh Suzanna," then had

Mary and Mrs. Rennie sniffling with "Home Sweet Home." He finished off with the hymn "Be With Me Lord."

When Gilbert and his family had gone home and Thomas had retired to his room for the night, Will poured a cup of tea from the pot that his mother kept going throughout the day. He sat with her in the kitchen. She had one hand clasped in the other and was rubbing a circle on her knuckles with her thumb. They were hands, Will knew, that rarely ever rested. A pall of melancholy had settled over her.

"I'm sorry, William. I cannot help myself. You will write often, won't you?"

Will nodded. His mother never used the diminutive of his name and always called him William, just as he always called her Mother. "You have my word. And with any luck at all, I might be able to slow Thomas down enough to drop you a line or two. I expect Gilbert will be preoccupied writing to Mary, but either Thomas or I should always be in a position to write." He reached over and laid his hand upon hers. "I know it's a mother's lot to worry, but try not to let it get the best of you. We'll be all right and come home as wealthy as kings."

"Your father and I had similar thoughts when we left England all those years ago. This was the Promised Land, too, just like those mountains you're going to." She paused, as if she had revealed too much. "We did all right, mind you, and I'm not complaining. But sometimes things have a way of not working out quite the way you expect."

"Well," said Will philosophically, "we still have to give it a try. A door to opportunity has been thrown open, Mother, and we'd be fools not to step through."

She nodded and sighed and looked her son in the eye. "The truth now, William. You've money to last, have you? I do not wish to insult you, but God forbid that you run short for want of asking."

Will smiled. His mother had been sent money from England after his father died, but she had not spent it, as Will and Thomas made more than enough to run the household. "I'm not insulted, Mother, and I appreciate your concern. We've plenty, thanks, and we're fully capable of any kind of labour if need be. My main concern is leaving you here to fend for yourself."

Will could tell that he had ruffled her feathers a bit, for she was an independent woman who deemed herself the family head and ignored her friends' urgings to take another husband. Her stock reply was always, "One was quite enough, thank you."

"I am quite up to the task," she said. "And there are plenty of neighbours around I can ask for help if ever I'm not."

Will would be surprised if she ever did. She was a strong woman, and he was as close to her as a son could possibly be to his mother. He wished that he could have said the same for his father. In fact, he and his father had always seemed to be at loggerheads, and he thought he knew the reason why. It stemmed from an incident when he was just five years old, one that he remembered with the clarity of spring water.

One night his father had stayed far too long in the public house and had come home in a foul mood. He and Gilbert were in bed when both were awakened by loud voices from the parlour. His parents were having an argument. He lay there in the dark, understanding little of the words flying between them, but frightened by their intensity. All of a sudden, there was the sound of a hard smack on skin, and he heard his mother cry out in pain. He did not know what came over him, but the next thing he knew he was downstairs, flailing away at his father's legs with his tiny fists and screaming at him to stop hitting his mother. She had pulled him away and he fell into her arms, sobbing. She carried him back to his bed and tucked him in. "There, there," she said, kissing his brow softly. "Don't worry. Everything's going to be all right." And it was.

From that moment on, he knew that his mother would never lie to him, because he heard no more noise for as long as he stayed awake. But he never trusted his father again, feeling that at any time he might have to protect his mother from those punishing blows. His father felt that lack of trust, but rather than try to close the gap between himself and his eldest son, he simply widened it further, bestowing what little love he was capable of showing on Gilbert and Thomas. To Will, his mother was the sun in a cold and empty sky, and she had always been there to provide warmth, to tuck him into bed, kiss his brow and assure him that everything was all right.

They sat for a while, chatting about things not connected with the trip, until his mother said, "You have a big day tomorrow. You'd best get some sleep."

He laughed. He had not heard that suggestion since he was a child going to school, but it was apt; he did not expect to get much rest on the train. His tea had turned cold, but he finished the dregs, placed the cup on the counter by the wash basin, and said, "Sleep well, Mother." He kissed her lightly on the cheek.

Glimpses into her heart were rare. She had steeled herself to a life that had not been easy, raising three boys and losing a husband and a daughter. Louisa, her third child, born two years after Gilbert, was 10 years old when a kick from one of the horses the family used to keep shattered her ribs and punctured her lung. There was little that the doctors could do for her. Will reckoned that it must be hard enough for a woman to bury her husband, let alone her daughter. He could not even begin to imagine what that must have felt like, knew only how badly it had devastated him. When he remembered his sister, he always tried to picture her smiling face, for she was a happy girl, but all he could see was her body laid out in a coffin, looking as fragile as a porcelain doll. He sometimes wondered what his mother saw.

He climbed the stairs to his room. They creaked underfoot as they always had and made him aware of yet another thing that he would miss. In bed, he tried to read more of Parkman's book, but there were so many thoughts whirling around in his head that he could not concentrate. He finally gave it up and blew out the lamp. He lay in the dark for a long time, listening to the sounds of the house as it contracted with the cooling night air. The last thought on his mind before he drifted off to sleep was hope that he was right and Thomas was wrong, that they were not leaving too late.

It was raining heavily when he awoke early the next morning. Inauspicious weather to begin a great journey, he thought, as he packed his bag with clothing, toilet articles, a few patent medicines as well as a herbal remedy or two that his mother had concocted, the maps and some oilskin to wrap them in and to protect his timepiece if need be. Lastly, he fitted in as much ammunition as he could. That done, he got his rifle from the wardrobe in his bedroom. It was a brand new, lever-action Henry repeater that the local gunsmith had ordered for him from the Volcanic Repeating Arms Company in Connecticut; it had arrived just five days ago. He had quickly made a leather case to protect it but could not help taking the rifle out to look at it. It was a thing of beauty with its polished wood stock, brass receiving chamber and blue-black barrel. It had cost him $42, a small fortune, but worth every penny as far as he was concerned, for it would last a lifetime as long as he took care of it. He put the stock to his cheek and aimed the gun at a mirror, pretending to squeeze off a shot. Whereas his old rifle had been a heavy and awkward muzzleloader — the type that Gilbert and Thomas were taking — the Henry weighed a mere six and a half pounds, which made it the perfect weapon for the coming journey. The brothers did not think that each of them needed one, and since Will wanted one the most, he happily bore the expense of the purchase. When he and Thomas had gone out to the back fields and set a target up for practice, both were impressed with the quick, smooth action of the weapon. Will was mildly piqued that Thomas could squeeze off shots faster and with more accuracy than he could. Then again, Thomas seemed more facile at many things.

He put the Henry back in the case and slipped it through the handles of the bag, with his small holdall of shoemaking equipment beside it. Now he was as ready as he would ever be.

By the time Gilbert arrived at 11 o'clock, the weather had cleared substantially and a warm May sun was drying things out nicely. The three brothers bade their mother goodbye. They would not allow her to accompany them to the train station, insisting that it would be too hard on her, but Will reckoned it was as much for their sake as it was hers. She hugged and kissed each of them in turn and wished them God speed, scarcely able to keep the tremor from her voice.

"Write as often as possible," she instructed. "Even when it isn't."

They left her on the front porch, dabbing at the corners of her eyes with her apron. Climbing into the wagon of a neighbour kind enough to give them a lift to the station, the brothers waved, but after that, Will did not look back.

Of the party of five going west, they were the first to reach the station, followed a few minutes later by Helstone and Wright. The first thing Will noticed was that four of them wore floppy-brim hats, good for keeping the sun out of one's eyes and the rain from going down the back of one's neck, but Helstone wore a short-visor cap that Will considered impractical. But along with a rifle, he also had a shotgun, and that was something that Will reckoned would probably come in handy.

Helstone was a loose-limbed, big man with slightly stooped shoulders and ponderous movements, more the type one would picture behind a plow rather than removing night soil and assisting patients at the hospital. A dark grey beard rimmed the lower half of a pinkish, lined face dominated by a large nose, and his blue eyes gleamed with what Will supposed was the same resolve that had sent him up to Montgomery's tavern with Fitzgibbon.

Wright was as different from his uncle physically as he was in personality. Slight of frame and of average height, he was fair-haired and handsome, with almost delicate features behind a sparse beard. His hat brim almost hid glistening dark brown eyes that always seemed to be on the verge of tears. There was a tic in the corner of his right eye that grew more evident as his nervousness increased. It would not have surprised Will if the young man had not shown up, for he never seemed very sure of himself. Then again, he had Helstone to spur him on, to drive him down roads he would not otherwise travel on his own.

Both men had brought their families to the station. Catherine Helstone was a quiet, rather attractive woman while Elizabeth Wright was plain and sober looking, each the opposite to the way Will had imagined them. The Wright daughters, one about five, the other still a toddler, were pretty things and Will felt a pang of envy and a hint of longing to have a family of his own.

Several people, friends and other well-wishers who had read of the impending journey, had gathered at the station to see them off. Will was surprised and pleased by the resounding cheer they received as they boarded the train at the last minute. He did not know how it affected the others, especially Wright who seemed to have the hardest time letting go of his wife and children, but it made him feel mildly heroic, enough to forget for the moment the apprehension that gnawed at his insides. The men had only just stowed their bags and rifles and sat down when a huge cloud of steam filled the platform and the train jerked away from the station, with Wright pressing his face against the window until the station disappeared from view. They gradually picked up speed and soon left the town behind, clacking past farms of newly planted fields, into the empty, verdant landscape, bound toward a line of clouds building in the west and Windsor, some 120 miles down the line.

CHAPTER TWO

JULY–AUGUST 1862

"My Dear Mother:

We have arrived at last in Fort Garry immensely pleased to find a letter from you awaiting us. We are relieved to know that you are faring well in our absence and give our assurance that you need not worry so much about us. We are in good health and are now in the throes of preparing for our plunge into the far west. This is a grand country, to be sure, so open and vast that no artist's brush or photographer's tintype could ever do it justice. I will tell you more about it later, for I would be remiss if I failed to first describe the journey that brought us here.

"The train ride to the Mississippi River was uneventful, though awfully tiring. Imagine, if you will, trying to get a good night's rest on one of your kitchen's hardest chairs as it lurched and swayed, and you will have some idea of what our nights were like! The steamer to St. Paul, though overcrowded, was luxuriously comfortable by comparison, thus I will refrain from complaining about the number of times it broke down.

"St. Paul would amaze you. What a busy town it was and much larger than I had anticipated, considering how far west it is. Pioneers and would-be miners, mostly greenhorns the likes of us five, have contributed to its growth and there is much wealth there. This wealth stems from everything being so shockingly dear. It seemed that every time we turned around we were opening our money belts. I suspect that if we had stayed long enough someone would have charged us for the very air we were breathing! Nevertheless, we were told things would be even more expensive in Fort Garry, if they were available at all, and thus handed our hard-earned cash over to the merchants of St. Paul to outfit ourselves. We purchased three oxen with carts and filled them up with a variety of food supplies from ham to tea and coffee, and various other items ranging from axes to lead shot for the shotgun. The tents we bought were nothing more than pieces of canvas that we had to sew together ourselves. I believe we did a commendable job, for the seams only leak slightly when it rains. Our bedding consists of blankets and buffalo robes that keep us reasonably dry when the tent does not.

"We set out then to walk to Fort Garry. Think of it Mother, 500 miles! Who would have thought that city men could walk so far? Nevertheless, we made reasonable progress despite the pace of Mr. Helstone who sometimes seems as sluggish as the rivers in this part of the world. Thomas shows little patience toward the man. (I can almost hear your thoughts, Mother, that surely it is not possible that there is someone more slow-moving than your oldest son, but I assure you, it is quite the case!)

"We had only been on the road for two days when the two Johns, Wright and Helstone, were injured after an ox ran off with one of our carts. Thank goodness, neither was seriously hurt, just cuts and bruises, and Helstone's hospital experience served both men well. He was able to dress their wounds without any help from the brothers Rennie. The cart, however, did not fare nearly so well. It broke into many pieces and held us up for two days while we repaired it. The ox was fine, although there was a moment when we considered turning it into food. They can be exasperating beasts at times, but we eventually learned their strange ways.

"We suffered another delay when Helstone twisted his ankle and forced us to rest up for a day. I expect we will get to know more of him in this regard, since he often leaps before he looks. Once he gets going, that is. I have never seen a man take so long to pack up and leave a campsite. He checks everything twice and on some occasions three times. This fastidiousness carries over into setting up camp as well, when everything has to be in its exact place, which everyone finds quite irritating.

"Young John Wright has proven to be a pleasant enough fellow who complains only about being so far away from home. He and Thomas, being the two youngest of the group, have become boon companions.

"Once we got going, the journey north from St. Paul was actually quite agreeable. The land was beautiful: soft, green hills with patches of birch and pine and dotted with lovely, clear lakes. We crossed the Red River at Georgetown, which was no town at all, only a pathetic collection of wood buildings owned by the Hudson's Bay Company. It is also the southern terminus for the steamboat to the colony, but as we had spent most of our money in St. Paul, we could no longer afford it.

"On the west side of the river, in the Dakota Territory, is a well-established trail that brought us here to Fort Garry. For miles it runs straight and true across a treeless plain as flat as the Thames. The horizon is the same no matter which direction one looks. Indeed, on cloudy days, had it not been for the steady course of the trail, and the Red River, it would have been most difficult to find north. And the silence on those plains once the wind has died is enough to make a man think that the entire world has deserted him.

"Luckily, we did not encounter a single Indian along the way. We kept a vigilant eye out and took turns standing watch throughout the night, for there was talk of war between the white man and the Sioux on the American prairies. Now we are here, safe in the long shadows of Fort Garry, a sturdy structure with massive stone walls twice the height of a man that would keep even the most persistent enemy at bay. It sits overlooking the confluence of the Assiniboine and Red rivers, both idlers much like the Thames. Beyond its walls is a cluster of houses and businesses owned by white families. Across the Red is St. Boniface, a sprawling community of Métis and a Catholic church, under construction, that will rival our own St. Paul's for size. The Métis own farms that front both of the rivers for miles. There are Indian encampments here, too — Assiniboine and Cree, I think — and remarkably, everyone gets along surprisingly well. So worry not, Mother. It appears as if the worst of the Indian threats is over and from this point on, we should be trouble free.

"I must leave you now. I will write upon reaching Fort Edmonton. Gilbert (you will be pleased to know that he is presently occupied writing to Mary) and Thomas send their deepest affections, as I send mine.

Goodbye from your loving son,
William"

Will wished that he could believe his own words, but truthfully, he was indeed worried about Indian attacks. However, there was no need to bother his mother with this information, particularly when there would be long gaps between letters. She would die from worry and lack of sleep. In fact, the letter from her that had beaten them to Fort Garry was full of concern for their welfare when they had not even begun the most challenging part of their journey. His mother worried far too much, and he needed to be careful about how much he revealed in his correspondence with her. In fact, he had not told her everything about the incident of the ox running off with the cart, for it had generated considerable tension within the group.

They had started out from St. Paul in high spirits, but as naïve as schoolboys about the oxen they had purchased. How to make them move, even, or stop once they got going. Sometimes the beasts would halt for no apparent reason, and it was during one of those episodes that Helstone lost his temper with his animal and began whipping it. In an attempt to escape the beating, the ox bolted. The right cart wheel thumped against a rock and split apart, flipping the cart on its side. The animal dragged it several yards, tearing off some of its boards and leaving a trail of supplies in its wake. Both Helstone and Wright had sustained scrapes and bruises when they unsuccessfully tried to stop it. The ox checked on its own as soon as it was out of Helstone's reach.

Fortunately, the men carried a spare wheel for each of the carts, but by the time the necessary repairs were made, they had lost the better part of a day. Everyone was angry with Helstone, particularly Thomas, who was seething. Fearing an altercation between the two men, Will stepped in to defuse the situation. "You had no call to do that, John," he said. "This is a dumb animal of a lower order than most and doesn't deserve to be beaten. You'll get more out of it by dangling a carrot than you will by whipping it."

Helstone's mouth moved as if he wanted to say something, but he thought better of it.

"I'll tend to our wounds," he said, and lumbered off and sulked for the rest of the day.

When he caused a further delay by twisting his ankle because he was not watching where he was going, Thomas had muttered to Will, "Good lord. We'll be lucky to make the goldfields by Christmas at this rate. You tell the man he's slow and he says that he's merely methodical. Methodical my arse."

"Go easy, Thomas," Will had replied. "It does none of us any good to have the two of you at odds with each other. Besides, the man's a born dawdler. That's just the way he's built and there's not a lot that you or anyone else can do to change him. You might as well get used to it. And I don't think it would hurt to show him a little respect, either. After all, he's old enough to be your father."

It was a demanding assignment, but under Will's watchful eye, Thomas reined in his impatience a bit. Nevertheless, a gap had developed between him and Helstone that neither man seemed willing to bridge.

Will sealed the letter to his mother and left it with the agent who assured him that it would go out on the next steamer to Georgetown.

The men did not dally in the colony. July was nearly a third gone and they needed to get a move on. Further inspiration came in the form of two priests, a lay brother, three nuns and their entourage, who were leaving immediately for the west, some for as far as Fort Edmonton. When the Hudson's Bay Company agent spoke highly of one of the priests, Father Albert Lacombe, and his considerable experience in the west, Will thought it might be wise to travel with them and told the others. They were eager to a man, except Helstone, who said, "Travel with a papist? What is this world coming to?"

He looked as if he had tasted something sour, but when Will told him that the Indians also held Lacombe in high regard, and that they might otherwise have to go to the expense of hiring a guide, Helstone came onside. Will went immediately to the priest and asked if he and his companions could join him.

"Of course," Lacombe said. "We would be honoured by your company and would ask only that you be self-sufficient." He went over some of the details about what to expect during the journey and the two men shook hands.

Their conversations came in spurts, like a flat stone splashing across a still pond. As each day passed, he turned more and more to his Bible, not so much to seek comfort there as to find answers to questions that plagued him about why these appalling circumstances had been visited upon him. In the middle of the night, he sometimes called out some half-remembered line; it rarely made sense and succeeded only in disturbing the others' rest.

They had been lucky enough to shoot one porcupine and a mink so far, both animals unwittingly passing in front of the campsite. The porcupine was tasty and the mink tolerable, but both added nicely to their rations. They sucked on the bones until they were shiny.

A general mood of optimism prevailed in the camp at first, and on the 10th day, the predicted day of their rescue, they all watched and listened with great anticipation, expecting at any moment that someone would appear or hail the camp. But no one came. Not that day nor the next, and it had now become demoralizing not knowing when or if someone was going to show up. They had to believe, though, that rescuers would eventually arrive, that at any moment they would hear them helloing from downriver. It was imperative that they believe, but he could see that the others were skeptical.

Will and the others traded their oxen in for fresh ones, and on Father Lacombe's advice, increased their provisions. They added more flour and ham, plus pemmican and that most important of commodities, tobacco for their pipes. Thus outfitted, they prepared for their departure the following day by visiting a drinking establishment in the village, little more than a spacious room added onto the owner's house. There were several rectangular tables with bench seats, a few filled with locals, but they found an empty one and sat down.

Will was in such a good mood, the result of hooking up with Father Lacombe, that he bought whiskeys for everyone. Helstone raised his glass in a toast. "To a changing world, boys. Who would have thought, fine Protestants that we are, that we would voluntarily put ourselves in the hands of a papist. My friends at home would never believe it."

Will wondered if he had any friends at home or anywhere else, for that matter. Like the others, he did not raise his glass. He was inclined to be suspicious of most things Catholic, but Helstone's remarks were uncalled for. If Helstone noticed the snub, he did not let on.

They all drank more than they should have, particularly Wright who became maudlin. Normally a reticent man, he spoke more easily under the influence of alcohol, pouring out words about Elizabeth, the children and home until Helstone halted him with, "You're whining, Johnny. No one wants to listen to you."

Will was tired of it, too, and noticed the tic in Wright's eye increase in speed. Nevertheless, the young man fell silent, which opened the door for Helstone to regale everyone with more grisly tales from his days working in hospitals. Some concerned astonishing wounds and botched surgeries, but the incident that most fascinated the others occurred when he worked at the mental asylum in Toronto.

"It had to do with a woman," he said, "who was somewhere in her 50s and crazy as a coot. She didn't respond to treatment, which was probably as good as you could get anywhere, but at least she was harmless. She called herself 'Mother Earth.' She loved to work in the hospital garden during the summer months and every winter she grew an imaginary garden in the common room. After a while, we noticed that she had begun to look physically ill, and there was an awful stench about her. She refused all help and would talk only about her garden. One day she fainted dead away and was rushed to the infirmary and examined by the doctor. He discovered straight away that her lower abdomen was swollen. Together we removed her underclothing, and the smell was sickening. The doctor examined her between her legs and said, 'Good God! Look at this!' Holding my nose, I looked and saw something green inside her. Carefully, the doctor extracted it. To our amazement, it was a potato! And it had obviously been in there for some time because there were tendrils of sprouts growing from it!"

While the others blanched, Helstone could scarcely contain his mirth. "It wasn't the least bit funny at the time," he added, "but the doctor said later that we ought to have sent the woman to Ireland where she might have single-handedly reversed the potato famine."

There was something to be said for a shoemaker's trade, thought Will, who did not like the story at all. He did not want to think about such things being in a woman's secret place, even a crazy woman. Though he had never paid a visit there, he had always imagined it being as sweet as honey.

And wasn't Helstone a curious fellow? Other than his size and self-righteousness, he looked every bit the ordinary person, not someone capable of turning such intimate knowledge of another into a joke. Will was perplexed and wondered how the man was able to find such an attractive wife. You certainly could not call him handsome, nor was he rich, at least not yet.

Later, returning to their tent near the confluence of the Red and Assiniboine rivers, Wright staggered and threw up most of what he had drunk. Thomas, in high spirits, helped him home. That was just like Thomas, Will thought, impatient about everything except birds with broken wings.

Since it was a warm evening and Will was not feeling particularly tired, he decided to walk down to the riverbank for a final pipe before turning in. A quarter moon was inching down the western sky and starlight reflected off the water in a murkier version of itself. He sat cross-legged in stubble that had not yet begun to gather dew, filled his pipe and lit it, shutting his eyes so that the flare of the match did not temporarily blind him. It was a fine night to feel so much in control of one's destiny.

Things were going quite well, he thought, despite the delay of having to walk from St. Paul to Fort Garry. They had originally planned to take a coach to Georgetown and the steamer to Fort Garry and outfit themselves there for the remainder of the trip, but local merchants had convinced them that it would be unwise. Fort Garry, they insisted, would probably not have what they needed, and if it did, prices might prove to be beyond their pocketbooks. It turned out not to be true, but they bought the story, spent 11 days outfitting themselves and left the bustling town on the Mississippi on May 28. It had then taken five weeks to cover the 500 miles to the colony. They had considered their average of 100 miles a week as making good time, but when Will told Father Lacombe, the priest was unimpressed. He said that cart trains did it in three to four weeks and they never travelled on Sundays. He then pointed out that it would probably take only six weeks to cover the 800 miles between Fort Garry and Edmonton. The insult added to the injury was that if they had not listened to the St. Paul merchants and had instead walked to Georgetown with only their personal belongings, then taken the steamboat to the colony, they would have been here two weeks ago.

At any rate, it did not seem to Will that he and his companions had been dawdling. Perhaps at first, but even Thomas had remarked that Will had improved his pace daily. He was grateful for the remark because he recognized the importance of penetrating the mountains before winter set in. So did Helstone, as far as that went, but Helstone was Helstone and always moved in his own peculiar way. It was quite apparent, though, that they had not been as quick as they might have. And it at least explained why a letter from his mother had arrived at the colony before them. In any case, they would be leaving Fort Garry tomorrow, July 8, and if Father Lacombe was correct, Fort Edmonton should be behind them sometime in August. That should still see them in the goldfields in time to put down stakes. Running into Father Lacombe was a definite coup, one of those strokes of good luck that made a man feel positive about his future.

Will was contemplating stuffing another plug of tobacco into his pipe when he heard the rustle of footsteps in the stubble behind him. A figure made its way toward him out of the darkness, a little wobbly, and he saw that it was Wright. The young man sat down beside him.

"My head was spinning," he said. "I needed air."

"There's plenty of it out here," Will said.

Wright sighed. "Sometimes more than a body really needs."

Wright had a way of wanting people to feel sorry for him, and Will was not up to it. Nor was he keen on hearing another of Wright's sob stories. You listen to too much of that stuff, Will thought, and it begins to rub off on you. He had told his mother that Wright was a pleasant fellow and that he and Thomas had become fast friends, but that was only to make his mother feel good. The truth of the matter was, Wright was a gloomy young man and Thomas pitied him more than anything else. Pity made a poor foundation for a friendship. What's more, the young man did not know his own mind, something that his uncle was quick to take advantage of. A request from Helstone was as good as an order for Wright, and Will did not care much for that either. It was almost as if the uncle had become the father the nephew hardly knew so he bent over backwards trying to please him.

All things considered, Wright cut a bit of a sorry figure, and because of that, Will was tempted to let the conversation die right there, forget about a second pipe, and go to bed. Instead, he found himself pulling out his tobacco pouch again. He filled his pipe and offered the pouch to Wright but the young man declined.

"I don't think it would be a good idea. Not the way my head and stomach feel."

Not really knowing what to say, Will stated the obvious, without knowing why: "You're missing your family."

"More than I thought possible," Wright said. "The drink doesn't help."

"Well, it'll soon be beyond your reach for a while, if that's any comfort."

Wright sighed again. "I suppose I should never have come in the first place. I was just getting used to Canada and now here I am in the middle of nowhere. A long way from England in more ways than one."

"Well, you could always turn back. Hook up with one of the cart trains that travels between here and St. Paul."

"I'd have a fine time living that one down."

Will didn't respond but reckoned that a swift kick in Wright's backside might do both of them some good. They sat in silence for a long while, listening to the frogs singing among the reeds edging the river. Will did not know much of Wright's background other than what he had been able to piece together during the trip up from St. Paul and at the tavern tonight. (It never ceased to amaze him how effective a glass of liquor or a flickering campfire could be in loosening a reticent man's tongue.) Back in the Old Country, his father, after trying his hand unsuccessfully at a variety of occupations, had ultimately turned to the whiskey bottle. He had gone off one night in a drunken rage when Wright was a lad and several days later, his bloated body was pulled from the Thames. Their house subsequently became a place that strange men, mostly drunkards and no-accounts, drifted in and out of and 10 years later, his mother died from lung disease. By then Wright had found Elizabeth. It was Will's opinion that the young man had sought solace in his marriage to her, for he was only 18 at the time and she was two years his senior. It was not a typical union, since men usually married women much younger than themselves. Will would have bet his first poke of gold that Wright and his family had left the Old Country at his wife's bidding, too; he would not have had the courage to do it on his own.

Wanting to find out more about Helstone, Will said, "Those were some stories your uncle told tonight. Especially the one about the potato."

"Yes. Well, that's Uncle."

"How did he meet Catherine?"

"At the hospital in Toronto. She was a patient and just about died from some strange illness." Wright looked back in the direction of the tent, perhaps to make sure that Helstone was not lurking about, then lowered his voice. "I don't know what he did for her there, but whatever it was she has always seemed obligated to him. I think that's why she married him."

Will nodded. He thought it might be something like that. They just didn't seem to fit as a couple.

Steering the conversation away from Helstone he asked, "What are you planning to do with your gold if you find some. *When* you find some, I should say."

Wright's spirit seemed to lift at the thought. "It's for Elizabeth, and Emily and Laura. I doubt that I'd be here if it wasn't for them. What about you?"

Will laughed. "I think I'll buy myself a luxuriously outfitted coach, a team of the finest horses to pull it, and never walk anywhere again. Then I'll hire my own personal shoemaker."

The moon gleamed as pinpoints in Wright's eyes and Will could vaguely make out the hint of a smile on his face. Since he would probably not find a higher note on which to end the evening than that, he stretched and said, "I'm turning in."

"Me, too," said Wright.

The two men returned to the tent and let themselves in as quietly as possible so as not to disturb the others.

CHAPTER THREE

JULY–AUGUST 1862

Two days were all they spent at the fort. At one o'clock in the afternoon on the third day, a little the worse for wear from the drinking the night before, they joined Father Lacombe's party on the sun-baked, cartwheel-rutted road outside the fort. At a signal from the priest, they headed into the open prairie, the oppressive heat of summer already at a suffocating, head-splitting intensity.

After several days on the trail, it became apparent that a blind man could have followed it. A large party of gold seekers that included about 150 people, nearly as many carts and more than 250 animals, had preceded them and churned the prairie into a road that was as traceable as a city street. In most places, it was a broad, dirty streak disappearing over a small rise or into the distant horizon. The only time it stopped was when it came to a river, but it was always there on the far side, beckoning the travellers on, and so they made good time despite the priests' insistence that Sundays be a day of rest and worship.

At first, Will and the others, except Helstone, balked at wasting a day on the trail, though they would probably have made a point of recognizing the Sabbath themselves had they left earlier and been on their own. Nevertheless, they soon learned to live with it. The opportunity of travelling with the experienced priest made the inconvenience worth it. And while the clerics conducted Low Mass for the nuns and Métis, those of the Rennie party so inclined said their own small prayers and then found something else to do. Helstone, and sometimes Thomas, would often spend this time with their noses in their Bibles, which Will considered a good thing, at least insofar as Helstone was concerned. It kept him occupied and out of harm's way.

Will held a fundamental belief in God but had little time for the trappings of the church. Raised a Presbyterian in the Free Church of Scotland, he had only attended back home because it was one of the things his family did on Sundays. Despite his protestant biases, he liked Father Lacombe. The priest was a congenial man in his 30s who was not afraid of hard work and getting dirt under his fingernails. He involved himself in every aspect of camp life, from setting it up at night to breaking it down in the morning, and he considered no task too menial. When Will commented on it, Lacombe simply said, "You'll never survive in this land by having other people do things for you. You've got to be able to do them yourself. Any man not willing to make the effort probably shouldn't be here in the first place."

He was familiar with the route they were on, having been over it a few times before, and was well versed in prairie lore. The Métis had been his teachers and from them he learned how to survive on the prairie, to tap resources that novices did not even know were there. He had travelled with them on their great buffalo hunts south of the international boundary when more than a thousand of them would bring down nearly as many animals. The Métis had also guided him as far north as the Peace River country and as far west as Jasper House. Such was his reputation that he was nicknamed the "black-robed *voyageur*." Born in Canada East, he spoke English with a heavy French accent, although his grasp of the language was excellent. He could also converse in several Indian dialects and was fluent in Cree, primarily because it was the trade language spoken around the Hudson's Bay Company forts. He was in the process of compiling a Cree dictionary and ran the mission at St. Albert, about 10 miles from Fort Edmonton. Will asked what had brought him to Fort Garry.

"It's been my belief for some time now," the priest said, "that the church should have its own freighting system. The Company has shipped our supplies from the east, and for a reasonable price, I might add, but the church has experienced a great deal of growth in the west and our requirements are now greater than the Company can handle. This brigade of carts is our first freight run."

Lacombe was visibly proud of his idea and revealed that while some of the supplies they were carrying were provisions for the mission at Lac La Biche, there were also gears, levers and a set of millstones for a horse-driven gristmill at his own mission at St. Albert. He added, "This return trip will be different for us in another way. In the past, we would only go overland as far as Fort Carlton and from there catch a ride with one of the Company *bateaux* going to Fort Edmonton. But since we are now our own freighters, we will make this journey entirely overland."

Will received that as good news. Even though the trail was obvious, to have the company of such a knowledgeable, experienced man all the way through to the fort was extremely welcome. Many a night beside the campfire, Will and the others asked questions of the priest who willingly supplied the answers. Uppermost in their minds was what the country west of Edmonton was like.

"The trail west of the fort, at least as far as the mission at Lac Ste. Anne, is fairly well established," said the priest. "That's about 30 miles. Beyond that, the muskegs are Hell on earth and can swallow up both man and beast in a trice if they are not careful. The rivers are colder and swifter than they are here, which makes the crossings more troublesome and dangerous. But that isn't all that should concern you. I was heading for the mountains with a small party once, to visit the Indians, when a forest fire near the Pembina River chased us down. I mean that literally — it had us on the run. A fire can spread through a tinder-dry forest as easily as it does over these grasslands. The flames leap from tree to tree with a swiftness that defies belief, particularly if there's a stiff breeze to help it along, and in that country there usually is. My companions and I had no choice but to take to the river, and we only just reached it in time. The fire roared by like a train, and the air was so hot that the water felt like a warm bath. Afterward, the land smouldered for two days and we couldn't move. It was like some form of Purgatory and the devastation seemed endless. So, a word of caution, my friends: light your campfires with great care and don't leave even the tiniest of embers in the ashes when you go. Another thing: it only takes one good lightning strike to turn the forest into a raging inferno. In either case, you'd better hope there's good place to hide that you can reach quickly.

"Naturally, the insects are every bit as aggravating there as they are here, perhaps even more so. Wait till you have to cross one of the countless muskegs out there and you'll know what I mean." He paused for a moment, choosing his next words carefully. "It's the kind of land you either love or hate. Few people are indifferent to it, simply because it demands so much just to survive it. And sometimes it isn't just the privation, work and fatigue that defeats a man; it's the sense of isolation, the sense of being so far away from the things that once gave him great comfort, including, *especially*, loved ones. Many a good man has broken down under the weight of that. As for me, it's in my blood and has been since I first gazed upon it. I can't think of any place else I'd rather be."

Will thought that he knew what the priest meant about the isolation. Even in the company of several other human beings, he felt it brush against his soul and could not imagine being totally alone. He was positive that the solitude and danger would drive him to do something that would ultimately cause more harm than good.

The other thing that concerned Will was that he and his brothers had never wanted for anything in their lives. Their father, though strict, had provided a good home for his family by dint of hard work; even when the town experienced lean times there was always an abundance of good food on the Rennie table. They had warm clothes on their backs and good boots on their feet in the wintertime. Admittedly, there were times when their father used a heavier hand than needed to inspire his boys to work harder, but they had never faced privation. Will hoped they never would.

On another occasion, Gilbert Rennie commented to Father Lacombe on the vastness and emptiness of the prairie. The priest responded, "You might think that but were I you, I would take a good look around as we pass." He stooped down and dug out a clump of soil with tough, meaty fingers. "This is what will change it, what will make it a land of abundance. Believe me, it will never seem so broad and empty again. Just as the movement of people up the St. Lawrence River was inevitable, so is movement into the west. Ultimately, it will be both blessed and doomed by settlement." He paused, a smile curving his mouth, then added, "Mind you, it's not something that the Hudson's Bay Company likes, of that you can be confident. They would prefer to maintain their monopoly and the delusion that God comes to them for permission before He proceeds with anything. But if they don't adapt, they will be swept away on the tide of change that has already begun to flood the land — much-needed change, I might add, that will make it a far better place."

They crossed the Assiniboine River in a Company scow that had seen better days and gained the high bluff on which Fort Ellice sat via a trail cut out of the side of a tributary valley. Beyond the fort was the Qu'Appelle River and beyond that the Touchwood Hills. Along the way, they saw the bleached bones of countless slaughtered buffalo scattered everywhere. They also saw Indians, off in the distance.

"They will be Cree," said Father Lacombe, "and pose no threat to us. They know that we are no threat either. They will be more concerned about running into a band of Blackfoot, although that's not likely to happen this far east. Beyond Fort Carlton, perhaps."

"They are enemies then, the Blackfoot and Cree?" asked Will.

"Yes. The Blackfoot feel the same way about the Cree as they do about white men and for the same reason. We are both encroaching on their land, which makes them quite belligerent at times. They've even threatened to burn Fort Edmonton down, but so far the worst thing they've done is destroy the crops around the post."

"Does the Company retaliate in any way at all?"

The priest raised his eyebrows. "Retaliate? It would not be a wise thing to do. The Blackfoot vastly outnumber the men at the post and could probably take it anytime they wished. The sensible thing to do is to try and stay in their good graces."

During the morning of August 8, the brigade crossed the South Saskatchewan River in a Company *bateau*. Here, Father Lacombe once again proved his worth. Saying to the nuns, "Mind your sensibilities, sisters," he removed his cassock, as the nuns tittered, and in his underclothing swam to the opposite bank to fetch the vessel. By suppertime, the brigade was trundling down the gentle slope, beneath a blistering summer sun, to Fort Carlton on the banks of the North Saskatchewan. As the next day was Sunday, they rested at the post before crossing the river and making for Fort Pitt. The other priest, Father Maisonneuve, could almost smell home.

Like Lacombe, Maisonneuve was an Oblate. He had been in the west for nearly a decade and ran the mission at Lac La Biche. He was a few years older than Lacombe and nowhere near as gregarious. In conversation he would often defer to his younger colleague, probably, Will thought, because his English needed serious work. Many of the carts in the brigade carried supplies for his mission. He was also taking with him a lay brother, a 21-year-old Irishman named Constantin Scollen. A serious young man fresh from the Old Country, he was always scurrying to ingratiate himself with the older priests.

The nuns would also be joining Maisonneuve. They were Grey Nuns from the Sisters of Charity in Montreal and kept pretty much to themselves. Will found them slightly mysterious in their heavy grey robes and the white wimples that tightly encircled their faces. Yet despite their femininity, he could find nothing the least bit attractive about them and wondered if he would if they shed their cumbersome clothing. Probably not. He guessed that they would still have an aura of sanctity about them that had nothing to do with their clothes and came instead from within. Once he looked up to find one of them staring at him with what he believed was compassion, and he wondered if she thought that he was a sour man because of his looks. He smiled at her, but she quickly looked away and did not say anything. Whenever the nuns spoke, it was usually in French, for their command of English was rudimentary.

Mostly, the nuns were a daily reminder for the married men of the party — Gilbert, Wright and Helstone — that they had left their wives at home. Wright seemed most affected by it. Will thought he might have pined away had he not been kept busy with the daily routine of making and breaking camp and keeping the animals moving in the right direction. They all missed their children, of course, but it was the comfort of their women that they longed for most. Since Will had never known the comfort of a close and intimate relationship with a woman, he could only imagine it. Thus far, his mother had been the only female in his life.

The brigade moved on with good speed, beholden to those who had gone before them and left many bridges in their wake. Though they were a welcome convenience for the Catholic entourage, they were especially important to the Rennie party with its greater need to make haste. The weather was mostly favourable too, and that helped, even if on some days it never quite seemed to know what to do, rain or shine. Often it did both at the same time. Regardless, the weather never held any secrets; its intentions were apparent for miles before it reached the cart brigade.

In a week they reached Fort Pitt, where Maisonneuve, Scollen and the nuns took their leave and veered off northwest to the mission at Lac La Biche. The rest crossed to the south bank of the North Saskatchewan and made a beeline for Fort Edmonton.

From this point forward, Lacombe and his Métis guide really proved indispensable. Most of the area around the Vermillion River, west of Fort Pitt, had been flooded when the main body of gold seekers went through, and there were few signs of their passage or of the faint trail that had previously been there. This was of no great concern to Lacombe and the Métis, who led the party unerringly through to Fort Edmonton and, furthermore, saved Will and the others the expense of having to hire their own guide.

Despite the priest's great value to the Rennie party, Helstone tried on more than one occasion to pick an argument with him. As a firm believer in the autonomy of congregationalism, Helstone disdained the hierarchical nature of the Catholic Church and readily expressed that opinion. Lacombe, however, always showed good sense in not rising to the bait even though it was apparent to everyone that he found the self-righteous Canadian annoying. Not only was the man an anti-Papist, he always seemed to be bringing up the rear — even his companions complained aloud of his slowness. Usually Lacombe did his best to ignore Helstone, but he would not let slide an accusation on their last night on the trail.

They were sitting around the campfire, the moonless sky a dome of flickering stars punctuated by gleaming planets. Everyone was tired from the day's travail but in high spirits, knowing that they would arrive at Fort Edmonton the following day. Lacombe, as he often did, spoke of the positive role that the Catholic Church would play in settling the land. Helstone interrupted and accused the church of being over-zealous in its drive to convert the heathen.

Apparently damning the consequences, Lacombe shot back, "It is no greater than the drive of some people to diminish our work. But we want only to put the 'heathen,' as you call them, on a path to heaven to which they are surely entitled. Furthermore, when your children and your children's children can travel this land without fear because the 'heathen' are living in pastoral contentment with plenty of food on their tables, it will be our

work here that will have to be acknowledged." Without giving
Helstone a chance for rebuttal, the priest stood up and added,
"We'll have an earlier start than usual in the morning. I want to
be at the fort by noon." Then he whirled and strode to his tent,
leaving an awkward silence around the fire.

He cut a notch in a stick for each day that passed since
the others left for the fort, and had just cut the 12th
one. They still had a bit of food left, some beaver tail
and moose meat, although they were limiting the rations
to finger-size portions about which he commented
dolefully, "I got more nourishment from my thumb
when I sucked it as a child." They had all lost weight;
their faces were gaunt, their frames turning angular
beneath their clothes, but at least they were not starving.
Twelve days though and still no sign of a rescue
party. Daily, he had gone to the beach with the spyglass
and scanned the shoreline downstream. He could see
about a third of a mile before the river bent away from
him. He kept the glass trained on the spot where the
river disappeared, expecting at any moment to see the
movement of a rescue party. He stayed there until he felt
the cold and his arms grew weary.
Though he tried not to let it affect him, there were
moments when he had to admit that the inclement
weather they had been experiencing day after day was
worrisome. A lot of snow had fallen since the others left
the camp and that would make traversing the shoreline
extremely difficult. Only God knew what the terrain
was like between here and the fort. What if there were
impassable land formations or rivers? The maps showed

none, but then they did not show any of the fierce rapids they had passed through either. Surely if their path had been blocked, the others would have returned by now.

The delay probably meant that the fort was farther away than they had assumed. That must be it. Yet sometimes, especially when his frostbitten feet bothered him and his companions were grumbling, depressing thoughts crept into his mind and he believed that help would never come, that he and his companions would not leave this awful place alive.

They reached Fort Edmonton on Wednesday, August 27, with the sun at its zenith. The post's complement was delighted with the return of Father Lacombe but paid scant attention to Will and his companions. The hundreds of gold seekers preceding them had rendered the quintet inconsequential. What's more, everyone was busy preparing for the pending arrival of HBC Governor Alexander Dallas and Chief Factor William Christie.

The biggest structure west of Fort Garry, Edmonton was laid out in an irregular pattern of six palisades of varying lengths, with four bastions. Inside the stockade were a number of log buildings and an incongruously large house erected by a previous factor that everyone referred to as the "Big House." A few shacks dotted the land nearby, many owned by Métis. A population of 150 souls shared the fort with countless dogs that roamed freely in the compound.

Will learned that there were miners working the North Saskatchewan about a half-mile upstream, so he went to see them, thinking that if the claims were producing, he might try to persuade his companions to winter here. He followed the shoreline of scrub bush and willows. The turbid river had subsided since the heavy summer rains and gravel bars poked up here and there. Overhead, white mare's tails streaked a blue sky. Rounding a bend in the river, he came upon a community of several hovels among which a few small sluices were in operation. He spoke with a man who introduced himself as Timoleon Love. Blond-haired and blue-eyed, Love hailed from Kentucky and was an exuberant individual who had rushed for gold on the Fraser River. More recently, he had led a small party of miners, known as the Saskatchewan Gold Expedition, from Fort Garry to Fort Edmonton. They had arrived at the post on August 8, and while some of them had pushed on for Cariboo, Love and a handful of others had stayed behind to search for gold in the North Saskatchewan. Will asked how he was faring.

"We're taking out about five dollars a day," Love said, "which is not bad considering that the labourers down at the fort only earn about 10 dollars a month. The problem isn't with finding gold; the problem is having to deal with the Hudson's Bay Company."

"In what way?" Will asked.

"The Company charges us outrageous prices for provisions and refuses to give us a decent price for our gold or anything else that we might have to sell. So they force us to trade directly with the Indians and then get annoyed when we do. They'd be happier if we all packed up and went somewhere else, mainly because they're afraid that we'll draw settlers to the area. They want furs and not much else."

Love's words reminded Will of what Father Lacombe had said about the Company's attitude toward anything that threatened the status quo. It helped make up his mind. It seemed pointless to winter here and get fleeced by an autocratic company when the real fortunes were awaiting them in Cariboo. *If we stay, we just might experience those privations that the priest talked about,* Will thought. *Better to take our chances in the mountains.*

"Well, I suppose we've little choice but to move on, then," he said.

Love looked surprised. "It seems to me that it's a bit late in the season to be crossing the mountains. It might be tough having to deal with the Company, but your chances of survival are probably better. It won't be long before there's snow up in those passes."

"We'll move fast. We're a small group, just five of us, and apparently there's no fear of losing the trail."

"Good trail or not, there's nothing easy about that route. I tell you that from personal experience. I've been over it. And if it snows, you'll find out how quickly it can disappear."

Will shrugged. "We ought to be able to make good time," he said with more confidence than he felt, because in truth, the thought of the mountains frightened him. Love described some of the trail and wished him luck. Will thanked the prospector for his time and returned to the fort.

He was just about to enter the main gate when he heard someone shout after him. Turning, he saw a sandy-haired young man, probably in his mid-20s, puffing up the trail at a trot toward him. The stranger introduced himself as Jim Carpenter and said that Timoleon Love had told him about Will and his party heading on to the mines. Could he join them? He had had enough of the Company's tyranny and was anxious to leave, but did not want to go on his own.

Will looked Carpenter up and down. Despite his fine features, the young man looked strong and capable and Will saw unmistakable intelligence in his dark eyes. It would not hurt to have an extra hand along in case complications arose, and he was sure his companions would concur. He stuck out his hand and said, "We're leaving in two days. If you can be ready that soon and my partners agree, you're welcome to join us."

"I'll be ready," said Carpenter. He smiled. "There's no fear of that!" He flew off, back down the path.

Will spoke to the others and, once they had decided as a group to go forward, all were agreeable to Carpenter joining them. They liked the idea of increasing their number on the leg through the mountains and accepted Will's assessment of him. Thomas went to seek out Carpenter to tell him of the group's decision.

The following day, cannons boomed out a welcome to the governor and chief factor as their York boat pulled in to the shore below the fort. That night, a gala affair in their honour was held in the ballroom of the Big House and, since it was open to all, Will and the others saw no reason why they should not attend. After all, they had been on the road nearly three and a half months now, and it would be a nice break from the daily rigour of putting miles behind them. It might also be their last opportunity to partake of such festivities for a long while.

The evening began with a feast in the ballroom of the Big House. Tables were full of roasts from a wide variety of game animals and birds — including moose and duck — along with mashed potatoes and other vegetables. Plum pudding and berry tarts were offered up for dessert, accompanied by tea or coffee. When dinner was done, which seemed to Will to be in the blink of an eye, the tables and chairs were cleared and pushed tight against the walls in order to leave as much space as possible for dancing. Small casks of rum and other liquors from which the guests could help themselves were set on the tables. Will noticed that Wright was extremely generous with the amounts he poured for himself and wondered whether the young man was inordinately fond of liquor or still needed to forget where he was.

The fiddles started up and the dancers took to the floor, mostly Métis and half-breeds for this first dance, which turned out to be a jig. Men and women formed separate lines facing each other, with a broad space between them. From the head of each line, a man and a woman met in the middle, joined hands and danced down the length of the lines and back again to their places, their feet moving so fast that Will could see no discernible pattern. The next couple repeated the process, and then the next, until everyone had had a turn. It was as energetic a dance as Will had ever seen, and he was not sure that he was doing it properly when his turn came. It did not matter. Those waiting in the lines clapped enthusiastically to the beat of the music and hooted and hollered good-naturedly when he stumbled.

It was splendid fun, but Will liked the slow dances best, when one of the Company men turned the fiddle into a violin by playing some dreamy English airs. Then he could be up close to his dancing partners and feel their femininity. He also loved the informality of inviting a woman to dance. All he had to do was motion toward the one he desired and, such was their love of dancing, not one of them turned him down.

Will and his companions danced the evening away with both Métis and half-breed women, for there was not a white woman anywhere in the region. Had Will been asked to consider such a possibility back in London, he might have balked. But this was the wild frontier and the women were fine dancers indeed and, more important, they were deliciously female. The bold colours of their attire were dazzling and exotic and they danced uninhibitedly, as if they had not a care in the world. Will found them exquisite creatures, wickedly erotic, and entertained thoughts of abandoning his quest for gold and settling here with one of them. He could scarcely recall the last time he had held a woman so close.

During a lull in the music, Will pulled Gilbert aside. Seeking reassurance in his own mind about the decision to carry on, he asked, "Any new thoughts about going for the mountains?"

Gilbert half-smiled. "Why? Are you worried?"

Will took a generous draft of rum that burned his throat on the way down. "I'd be both a liar and a fool if I said I wasn't." He wondered if he could have said that without help from the rum. "Aren't you?"

His brother shrugged. "Well, I'd feel a whole lot better if you and me and Thomas were on our own. Wright should have stayed home and his uncle can drive a man to drink." As if to reinforce what he had just said, Gilbert took a long swallow. "But we've made it this far with them so I suppose we can make it the rest of the way. If the weather starts turning on us, though, and Helstone doesn't pick up the pace, I think I'd be inclined to leave him behind."

"We can't do that, Gilbert. If anything ever happened to him … " He left the possibilities to his brother's imagination. "We'll want to go home sooner or later."

"Well, you asked what I think. Now you know."

That I do, Will thought. But what do I do with it? The notion of arguing with his brother about leaving Helstone behind in inclement weather set his stomach to churning. Then again, Gilbert might have been joking; it was often hard to tell with him. "I'll talk to you later," he said, and went to seek out Thomas who he knew would be full of enthusiasm and positive thoughts about the coming days. But someone had pulled out a concertina, and it had found its way into Thomas's hands.

Under normal circumstances, Will was certain, Thomas would not have had the nerve to perform in front of so many people, but the rum and the unqualified encouragement of everyone made him bold. People shouted requests at him but most were unfamiliar. Then Will called for "Billy Barlow" and everyone clapped along in time and, once they picked up the words, sang on the chorus: "Oh, oh, tragedy oh! Now isn't it hard up on Billy Barlow."

After the singing, they danced some more, until the musicians could no longer play and the energy had gone from the crowd. People left in couples and in groups, and Will and the others headed back to the tent, singing most of the way. Again, Thomas helped Wright down the path because he was unsteady on his feet. Will had never felt more alive in his life. He felt an intense confidence surge through his body, whiskey-driven perhaps, but no less real for it. They were an odd group, he and his companions, but they could do this thing, they could pull it off. He was absolutely convinced of it at this perfect moment in time. His euphoria was heightened when Thomas and Wright tripped over a root and did a strange dance as they tried to regain their footing, then, with everyone laughing madly, plunged headlong into the scrub bushes at the side of the path.

Will dreamed that night of a woman dressed in a kaleidoscope of colours who came to him, mouth turned up to meet his. He took her in his arms and pulled her to him, until he was so lost in her colours that it was impossible to tell where he ended and she began. He awoke in the morning on his stomach, pushing hard into the ground. He wondered where the drums were coming from, then realized that it was merely the dull throb of a headache. His mouth was as dry as prairie dust. He would have gladly transported himself back to that sublime evening or, better still, to his dream, instead of having to face the treacherous road ahead.

The afternoon found them all still slightly hungover, a few miles northwest of the fort on the St. Albert trail. They were now six men, five oxen and one packhorse, with no one to rely on but themselves. Near Big Lake they passed Father Lacombe's mission but did not stop. The priest had stayed behind at Fort Edmonton, having business to attend to, and had wished them Godspeed and good luck in their search for gold. Now they could see his church, an elongated, whitewashed building of sawn timber with a small cross jutting up from the roof's ridge. It had a place of prominence on a hill above the Sturgeon River near where the river flowed into the lake. Will's admiration for the black-robed voyageur had increased daily during their long passage across the plains. The man certainly knew what he was about in a land that had little time for folly and none at all for mistakes. He would miss Lacombe's company, but most of all, he would miss his knowledge and experience.

They crossed the river, over the bridge that the priest said he had helped build, and turned west into the immense tract of spruce forest and bogs stretching toward Lac Ste. Anne and beyond to the Rocky Mountains. It's a bold move this, Will thought. Or a foolish one.

Chapter Four

September 1862

The packhorse nickered and its ears pricked up as it stopped dead in its tracks, bringing the oxen and men behind it to a halt. Thomas was leading the animal, and he motioned to his companions to hold still. He went as swiftly and quietly as he could to a small hummock beside the trail and crept to the top. About 80 yards off, standing right in the middle of the trail, was the biggest buck he had ever seen. Being upwind, it had not heard the small party's approach. Thomas returned to the group as silently as he could. He held a vertical finger to his mouth to signal that he wanted silence, then stuck extended thumbs to his temples with his fingers up in the air to represent antlers. He motioned to Will that he wanted the Henry. Will removed the rifle from its scabbard on the packhorse and levered a shell into the chamber. The action made a loud "click" and the brothers winced. Will handed the Henry to Thomas, who returned to the hummock.

The deer had moved off to the edge of the trail, its head up, sniffing the wind, but there was still an opportunity for a good shot. Thomas carefully aimed the rifle, annoyed at the slight tremor in his hand. He was squeezing off the shot when the deer sensed the presence of danger. It bolted. The blast of the gun shattered the silence of the wilderness and Thomas saw the animal lurch. Then it was gone, crashing through the forest.

"Damn it!" He was confident that he had hit the deer, but how far into the forest had it run, and was it hit badly enough to stop? It was not as if they needed the food, but the thought of fresh venison was tantalizing. Eating pemmican day after day was merely subsistence and did nothing for the palate. Granted, they had had a good taste of fresh fish and vegetables a few days ago at the Lac Ste. Anne mission, but there was nothing like a few meals of pemmican and bannock to make a body forget that good food ever existed.

Will and Thomas followed the trail left by the buck, blazing the trees as they went. About 200 yards in, they came upon the animal, panting and in a state of near-collapse. Thomas held out the Henry to Will.

"Finish it off," he said.

But it was Thomas's kill, and he was clearly excited about it. Will shook his head. "It's yours. You do it."

That was all the permission Thomas needed. He quickly raised the rifle and put a bullet into the beast's brain. It crashed to the ground. Will went back to fetch the others.

Helstone was the only one among them who had field-dressed a deer before, and he instructed them to turn the animal on its back and prop it up with fallen limbs along each side. With his knife, he removed the genitalia, then made a vertical slit from high between the animal's legs down to the pelvic bone. He inserted two fingers into the top of the cut to hold the skin and meat away from the entrails and stomach and, turning the sharp edge of his knife blade up, slit the deer open right to its jaw. He was careful not to go too deep because piercing the intestines or stomach would cause a smelly mess. He severed the windpipe at the top, grabbed it with both hands and pulled downward with all his might. The insides, all the way to the mid-section, came out. Removing one of the logs, they turned the deer over on its side and Helstone cut away the thin layer of meat that attached the entrails to the ribs. After repeating the process on the other side, he gripped the slippery entrails with both hands and, once again, pulled down hard to remove them. While two of his companions held the deer's hind legs open, Helstone cracked the pelvic bone apart and removed the remainder of the insides. They carted the carcass out to the main trail, found a good place to set up camp, and hung the deer by its antlers to drain the blood from it. Meanwhile, Helstone skinned the animal while it was still warm, making the process easier.

Will had a good fire blazing; each man cut himself a hefty chunk of meat and roasted it for dinner. They dried what they could and in the morning packed as much undried meat as could be eaten before it became flyblown. They left the rest for the carrion eaters and rejoined the trail west, as obvious through the forest as it had been over the prairie.

It had been no picnic getting to the Pembina River, the first major crossing on this leg of the journey. Beyond Lac Ste. Anne the trail ran through bog after bog. Father Lacombe had called them "Hell on earth," but the men now considered that a gross understatement. The trail that the main body of gold seekers had left behind was in most places a blessing, particularly in the blow-down areas where it had been hacked through the jumble of trees. In the muskegs, though, it was a curse. The badly churned-up mud made travel excruciatingly slow and arduous. Will lost track of the number of times he sank in mud above his waist, and the oxen and the horse were often in so deep that he wondered if they would ever get them out. And how many times had they unloaded and loaded the packs? Too many to contemplate. Everyone was cut, bruised and sore, and though no one said as much, Will would not have been surprised to hear that they all had sporadic thoughts of turning back, just as he had. But how could they? There was only one direction to go now and that was forward. Thank God, the animals were holding up to the incredible strain placed upon them.

Once they reached the Pembina River, they forded it by letting the animals swim to the far bank while the men hung onto their tails, a task faced with some trepidation by Helstone and Wright, neither of whom had much confidence in their swimming abilities. The brothers and Carpenter returned to the far side without them and, over several trips, floated their supplies across, using the canvas tent as a protective covering.

Will and Gilbert were making the final trip when Will's fingers grew so numb that he could not hang on to the pack. Gilbert could not hold it by himself in the current and let it go. The others looked on in horror as some of their rifles, axes and food went floating off in their tent. Luckily, the pack got hung up in a snag a quarter of a mile downstream, on the near side of the river so that it did not have to be floated across again. Helstone and Wright were able to retrieve it, but the incident reminded everyone just how tenuous their existence was in this country.

Will apologized to the others. "I'm sorry," he said. "I should have been more careful, but my fingers got so numb I lost my grip."

It was a poor excuse since everybody's fingers were numb. He should have tied a rope to the pack and then wrapped it around his arm. Though no one called him on it, he felt bad. The loss of the pack would have been serious enough to force them back to the mission at Lac Ste. Anne, if not Fort Edmonton.

Thomas said, "Don't worry about it, Will. It wouldn't have happened if everyone was pulling their own weight."

The barb made Wright blush, but Helstone appeared unfazed. That was typical, thought Will. The man operated in his own small world and seemed oblivious to much of what was going on around him.

Except for Helstone's frequently irritating behaviour, the men functioned reasonably well as a unit now that they were on their own. Will had become the de facto leader, if for no other reason than that he made sound decisions. Not as quickly as the others would have liked — particularly Thomas — but then, few things could quell his impatience to get where he was going. Nevertheless, Will and Thomas were getting along as well as they ever had. The sense of camaraderie reminded Will of when Thomas was small and the two would go swimming or skating. To Will's relief, the late departure from London seemed to have been pushed to the back of Thomas's mind, for he no longer mentioned it. Presumably it was because he was as caught up in the adventure as the rest of them and it now looked as though they would reach the goldfields before winter.

No one was more grateful for the lack of squabbling than Gilbert, who faced each day's trials and tribulations with his usual aplomb. Will appreciated his brother's quiet confidence and valued his presence more than anyone else's. He could not imagine being on this trip without him.

Though it had taken a while, Wright had settled into the journey. At the beginning, scarcely a night went by around the campfire that he did not lament the leaving of Elizabeth and the children, but as the days wore on, he spoke of them less frequently. He stopped for good after Helstone, in a churlish mood, chastised him. "For God's sake, Johnny," he said. "Quit your damned moaning. We all have loved ones that we miss." The malleable Wright did as he was told and any objections he may have had were confined to a few extra tics in his eye.

The new addition to their party, Jim Carpenter, had proved to be an asset. A lawyer from Toronto who fancied himself an adventurer-explorer, he was clearly enjoying the challenges of the journey. "I'm just as happy to be here as in an office back home," he told Will and the others. "A man can practise law pretty well anywhere and at any age, but he can't always do this. Besides, Toronto is getting too big and growing too fast for my liking." He worked hard and never had to be told what to do. Will found it difficult to believe that Carpenter and Wright were the same age; the lawyer, with a better grasp of who he was, seemed much older and wiser. He was a good man to have along as far as Will was concerned.

After crossing the Pembina, they camped one night near a lonely gravesite, the occupant of which, according to the marker, had died nearly two years before. Carved in a nearby tree was a much fresher inscription: "A hard road to travel," which Will presumed was the handiwork of those who made this trail. Thanks to their hard work, Will's and the others' was that much easier. The discovery of the grave touched them all, particularly Wright who passed the entire evening quiet and melancholic, the tic in his eye quickening to a lively pace.

More days of gruelling work got them to the McLeod River. Fortunately, it was not running too high and they were able to find a decent ford. But the swift water felt near freezing and took their breath away as they led their animals across, and the bottom was treacherous with slippery stones. Everyone was tense as Helstone and Wright crossed, especially Helstone, because if anyone was going to slip and fall victim to the current, he would be the one. It was not until he was out of the water and climbing up the west bank that they all started to breathe again. He was the last to cross, of course, just as he was last at everything.

They moved through vast tracts of spruce forest and muskegs and into the foothills, always grateful for the work of their predecessors. The mornings were colder now, and the men usually shivered until they got moving. When it rained, they were miserable and cold, and sometimes it seemed to take forever to get a fire started. One morning they could not get one going at all and had to do without their tea. That left everyone in a bad temper. But at least the rain and the cold kept down the insects, which, during the afternoon and early evening, were voracious and frequently attacked the men and animals in dense swarms.

The party reached the Athabaska River and veered away from its unspoiled beauty to follow Maskuta Creek. On the very threshold of the mountains, they were awed by their sheer size. None of the men had ever seen the likes of them before. Helstone, who said he had travelled among the Welsh Cambrian Mountains, commented ruefully that they were not really mountains at all next to these giants. It was like comparing mice to men.

The deeper they penetrated into the range the tighter grew the knot in Will's stomach. One bitterly cold morning they awoke to a world that seemed more silent than usual. Will poked his head out of the tent and looked around in utter disbelief. Six inches of snow lay on the ground. In other circumstances, it might have been a sight of stunning beauty, but not now, not when time was beginning to slip away from them. He recalled Timoleon Love's warning and thought, my God, what have we got ourselves into? Maybe they should have stayed at Fort Edmonton and put up with the high-handed tactics of the HBC.

They passed the great massif of Roche Miette and followed the slender trail that skirted Disaster Point before rising nearly 2,000 feet along the mountainside. Fortunately, the weather had moderated and the trail was free from snow. But it was precipitous and barely wide enough for the animals. From the highest point, the Athabaska River and its tributaries looked so small it made Will think of the tiny rivulets he used to make as a child, dragging a twig through the mud on the banks of the Thames. He reckoned that a climb of only a dozen yards more would have put them in the clouds, which to his mind might have been a blessing. He had never been fond of heights and looking down made his knees weak. He breathed a huge sigh of relief when they were back beside the river again.

They built a raft and crossed the Athabaska, leading the animals behind them, tied to each other like a string of fish. On September 28, they began a terrible passage through the Miette River Valley up to the Yellowhead Pass. They had to ford the Miette several times and the water felt like the Thames in the dead of winter. The men had never been in water so cold for so long, and at one ford, where the water was chest deep, it sapped their strength completely and nearly swept them away. Once in the heart of the pass, they were only 40 miles or so from Tete Jaune Cache, the point where they would leave this treacherous mountain range behind once and for all. And that was the only good news.

They wove their way along the forested shores of Yellowhead and Lucerne lakes and camped beyond them. In the morning they had gone a full mile when Helstone realized that he had left his pipe back at the campsite. He said that he could get by without many things on this journey but tobacco was not one of them. He was going back to get it.

"We're not waiting for you," Will said. "We'll meet you at the next camp." His split-second decision echoed the feelings of the others except Wright, who seemed uncertain.

"Shall I go back with you, Uncle?" A question more out of duty than concern.

Helstone shook his head. "There's no need to, Johnny, I'll be fine." He tethered his ox, took his rifle and began retracing his steps.

The others stood and watched until he disappeared from view, then continued on. Will wondered what they would do if Helstone failed to show up. After all, any number of things could happen to him, falling and breaking a leg being a prime example. Then what would he do? Would anyone go back and look for him? Gilbert wouldn't, Will knew that, but what about himself? He honestly could not say, but it was relief he felt and not disappointment when Helstone eventually caught up with them. They had just set up camp on a gravel bar along the Moose River when he "helloed" them.

A cold rain began to fall, lightly at first, then in a thick, drenching downpour like the heavy rains that accompanied summer thunderstorms back home. They could see nothing around them except rain, which continued throughout a long and miserable night, great volumes of water sheeting down onto the tent and seeping through the seams. It was impossible to stay dry, and they awoke in the morning to find that the river had risen so high it flowed all around them; their campsite was now on an island.

The new stream made by the rain was swift and muddy, so they could only guess at its depth. They discussed the best course of action and decided that Helstone, being the tallest, would tie a safety rope around his waist and try wading across. Gilbert trimmed a long, slender piece of driftwood into a pole that Helstone would use for balance and to test the depth. Slowly he waded in, the cold water rising above his knees, then the shock of it in his crotch. By the time he was waist-deep he was having trouble keeping his footing and needed to rely on the pole for support. He dug it into the bottom with each step and with each step, the stream wanted to carry it away. When the water reached his armpits, he lost his footing and the current grabbed him. The others quickly hauled him back to shore, sputtering, while the pole was carried off downstream.

"We'll never make it across," Helstone said through chattering teeth. "It's too bloody dangerous."

Will looked at the sky. It had finally stopped raining, but he saw no signs of clearing. Ragged grey clouds sagged ponderously into the valley, obscuring the surrounding mountains and reducing the visibility to less than half a mile.

"We'll wait," said Will. "If the rain holds off for a while the water is bound to subside."

"What if it doesn't?" This was Carpenter, long-faced. He had awakened feeling feverish and in a dismal frame of mind.

"We'll worry about that when the time comes," said Will. "Meanwhile, we should wait."

They collected every piece of driftwood they could find on their tiny island, all of it wet, and got a fire going. They had to keep it small so that the wood would last, but it was enough to boil water for tea. They ate some pemmican and waited patiently throughout the day. With nothing to forage on, their animals went hungry. By bedtime, it had not rained and the stream appeared to be subsiding. Retiring with their fingers crossed that it would not rain during the night, the men awoke to a dry morning with the river down enough to allow fording. But Carpenter had been feverish throughout the night again and was so sick he did not want to move.

"You'll have to move enough to get off this island," Will told him. He felt both sorry for the man and annoyed. The last thing the party needed was someone getting sick, particularly in a place like this.

"It's all right. Leave me here. I'll catch up with you."

"If we leave you here, you might not survive to catch up with anybody. You're coming with us."

Groaning, Carpenter dragged himself out from between his blankets and out of the tent. He complained of a vicious headache and said his chest felt as if one of the Rocky Mountains was on top of it. He sat off to the side, huddled in a blanket, while the others packed for him. They left the packs off the horse so that Carpenter could ride it over without getting wet and, once across, Gilbert and Thomas returned to the island with the animal and retrieved the packs. They moved only a mile or so down the valley, to a spot with good forage that was in no danger of flooding, and camped there.

The next morning they forged on. Carpenter's fever had broken but he was still feeling wretched and now had a bad cough, although he pronounced himself well enough to travel. A good thing, Will thought, because their food supply was almost gone. It was serious enough that when a crow landed near camp, looking for a scrap of food, it became food itself. Thomas shot it, but it was lice-ridden and, once plucked, made a skimpy meal.

The boulder-strewn shore of Moose Lake was pure agony to negotiate. The party painstakingly picked its way over jumbles of small boulders that could easily trap a leg and snap it in two. Some were so huge that they could only be bypassed by wading through the frigid water. This went on for 10 miles. To add to their misery, the men worried about their animals' ability to cross such rugged terrain and were alarmed when one of the oxen began bleeding at the mouth. They could only hope it would survive until at least the end of the lake as this was no place to butcher it. Worse, the loads of the other animals would have to be increased, and they were already finding the task demanding. With great care, men and animals inched along the shore, expending more energy per step than they had anywhere else on the entire journey.

Yet as bad as it was for Will and the others, it was pure hell for Carpenter, particularly when the party had to take to the water around impassable points of land. He seemed to take forever to regain his body heat and stop shivering, and needed to stop at short intervals to rest. He had become as bad as Helstone with his constant delays and the feelings among the others about him ranged from compassion to resentment.

When they at last reached the end of the lake, Will could hardly believe they had done it without serious injury to man or beast. They were now only 18 miles from Tete Jaune Cache, but it would be a long 18 miles, for the food they had left was scarcely enough for a child let alone six grown men. Five, actually; Carpenter had no appetite whatsoever.

That night in camp, exhausted though they were, the men decided to butcher the ox that had been bleeding. Gilbert shot the animal through the head and Helstone expertly dressed it. The smell of its succulent meat roasting on the fire was painfully tantalizing and no one could wait until it was fully cooked. The men ate rare beef until they could eat no more.

With full bellies and the Cache within striking distance, they were in good spirits for a change. After their meal, they sat around the fire smoking their pipes and telling stories of home. Helstone was inspired enough to tell a few more stories of life at the mental asylum. Will listened, fascinated. Say what you will about the man, he thought, he was a mesmerizing storyteller. You had to give him that. And no one paid more attention than his nephew, who hung on every word.

In the morning, they did not waste time drying the remainder of the meat. Instead, they wrapped it in the deerskin, loaded it on another animal and struck out at once for Tete Jaune Cache.

They descended quickly through the valley of the Fraser River, where the deadfall had been cleared away by their predecessors, and traversed a broad talus slope along a trail that had been recently cut. It was narrow, and one false step would have brought certain death, but they crossed with caution and reached the far side without mishap. Once the valley had swung southwest and the glacial peak of Mount Robson loomed behind them, Will knew they had not far to go if what Timoleon Love had told him was correct. Still, nightfall caught them up and forced them to camp short of their goal. By noon the following day they entered the Robson Valley, wide and forested, in which Tete Jaune Cache was located. It was October 4, and the leaves of the huge cottonwood trees had turned yellow-brown and begun to fall. The weather, though, was mild as summer.

He thought a lot about dying and he supposed his companions did too, but they did not share their feelings with him. He guessed that to express such thoughts aloud was tantamount to admitting that they were doomed.

One particularly nasty night, when the wind howled out of the north and the snow flew as thick and impenetrable as a wall, piling up in drifts so high they could no longer see the river from their shelter, they

gathered as close as they could to the fire for the little
warmth that it gave. Despite the windbreak they had
built around the pit, sparks flew helter-skelter, shooting
up into the trees to die there. A feeling of immense
power surged through him like a gust of wind, causing
him to reach out from beneath his blanket and, in
a voice that rivalled the wind, command, "Give me
your hands!" The firmness and strength with which he
spoke took his companions by surprise, and before they
knew what they were doing, their hands were reaching
out from beneath their own blankets for his. He took
them in his grasp and led them in a prayer of his own
devising, saying that if only they believed, God, in his
infinite mercy, would deliver them safely from this
camp. Afterward, though, he wondered about himself.
Where had that come from? He had few doubts that the
prayer had comforted his companions, but he worried
that his own mental faculties might be slipping.

They had hoped to find an HBC post. Instead there was only
a small band of Shuswap Indians camped at the river's edge. All
around was a scene of devastation left behind by the main party of
gold seekers that had passed through a month before. The bones
of oxen slain for food were scattered everywhere, and the forest in
the vicinity had been all but decimated to provide logs for their
huge rafts and dugout canoes. Despite these conditions, it was
cheering to have arrived. The Rocky Mountains, the obstacle
they had feared most, were behind them now and from this point
forward the journey to Cariboo would be comparatively easy.
They reckoned that the canoe trip down the Fraser River should
not take more than two weeks.

The first thing the men did after setting up their own camp was barter with the Natives for food, mainly berry cakes and smoked salmon. Will was also able to obtain a moosehide that would probably serve many useful purposes, not the least as a rain cape. Noticing Carpenter's cough, one of the Natives gave him some ointment, indicating that it came from the cottonwood tree and that he should rub it on his chest. Helstone advised the young lawyer to throw it away as he did not trust the Indians and feared it might do more harm than good. Carpenter did not agree. None of his patent medicines seemed to work and he was willing to try anything. The ointment gave him modest relief.

The next thing the men did was begin work on two dugout canoes. They had to search deep in the forest for suitable trees and eventually found two cottonwoods with straight trunks that were limbless for the first 30 to 40 feet. It took more than a week to fall the trees, trim the bark and fashion them into canoes, one 25 feet in length, and the other 20. The painstaking process of hollowing them out with adzes was tiresome, so they spelled each other off. Those who were not working on the canoes slaughtered the oxen for food. Without giving any thought to how long it would take to carve the canoes, they killed all the oxen at once. This proved to be a mistake, for some of the meat spoiled in the unseasonably warm weather before it could be dried. They did not think it was anything they should be concerned about, however. The consensus was that they had more than enough food for the trip downriver.

The good weather caused other problems, too. The blackflies were horrific. The men had brought nets to hang over their hats to protect their faces, but if there was an opening anywhere, the tiny pests found it. Sweat particularly seemed to attract them, and as the men worked in the small clearing, cries and blasphemies mingled with the thud of axes and adzes. They built several smoke fires to keep the flies at bay and by each day's end, they were all red-eyed and coughing.

By October 14, the canoes were finished and the men had now to face the daunting task of hauling them to the river, a full mile away. They carried and dragged the cumbersome vessels over the deadfall and stumps blocking their path, backbreaking work that took most of the day.

Meanwhile, all the beef had been dried and supplemented by more smoked salmon. The Indians eagerly traded away their food, which to them was easily replaceable, for such items as clothes, needles and thread. They also wanted ammunition, and since the men had had little need to use their weapons, they gave up a good supply of it.

Will was curious about how the Indians fished, and one day, during a break from meat-jerking duties, went to watch them. They used an ingenious latticed channel and cage that trapped the fish once they had swum into it. Will was impressed. He watched them pull salmon of unbelievable size from the cage, guessing a few weighed in excess of 50 pounds. The Indians beheaded and gutted the fish and left them to dry for a couple of days in the sun. Then they removed the spine and vertebrae and skewered the flesh to hold it open. A combination of sun, air and smoke cured the meat to the point where it would keep indefinitely. Will thought it was delicious, far superior to jerky in taste and nowhere near as tough.

The Indians fascinated Will. They were human beings in every respect, he thought, except for their inability to create civilization. It struck him as odd, for they were intelligent creatures who understood their environment to an extent that he could only envy. Nowhere was this expertise more evident than in their use of the cottonwood tree. They used its wood to make friction fire starters, converted its inner bark into soap and, because it was excellent firewood, they burned it and used the ashes to clean their hair and buckskins. And these particular Indians, at least, seemed quite willing to get along with white men, too. Yet Will and the others considered their primitive nature akin to a wild animal's and for that reason alone did not trust them. That was why they had set up camp a safe distance away and posted a watch. They feared being robbed and possibly killed while they slept.

On their last night at the Cache, the men pored over the map they had of the Fraser River. What they beheld was a thin, wiggly line trending to the northwest between stylized mountains before it turned south to Fort George, the first outpost of civilization from the Cache. The fort was marked on the map, as was Quesnellemouth, where the Quesnel River joined the Fraser another 90 or 100 miles farther downstream. This was the jumping-off place for the road to the goldfields. Without taking into account the myriad bends in the river, the overall distance was nearly 300 miles. They thought they could easily make 30 miles or more a day, which would see them at their destination in 10 days. Even a paltry 20 miles a day should see them there in a couple of weeks. Still, Will wondered what sort of knowledge, if any, the Indians had about the river, and wished he could ask them.

He folded the map and put it away, knowing full well that just as money was only symbolic of real wealth, the map was only a symbol of the territory and had little to do with the real thing. Nevertheless, he and the others went to bed with high hopes that the river was a friendly serpent, twisting its way through the mountains, that would take them swiftly and safely to Quesnellemouth.

Except for their turn on watch, they slept the restful, dreamless sleep of the innocent.

Part Two

THE RIVER

CHAPTER FIVE

OCTOBER 1862

They lashed the bulky canoes together, side by side, to give them greater stability. Will whistled as he worked, filled with optimism. Indeed, spirits were high all the way around as the others also went briskly about their work; even Carpenter was in a better mood now that they would soon be underway again. The weather was still mild, although a mackerel sky suggested a change. Finished with lashing the canoes, Thomas solicited help from the Indians to manhandle the heavy weight into the water. The Indians talked amongst themselves all the while, and the way they looked at Will and the others, he thought that they were probably saying something akin to "Crazy white men!" It was as if they were privy to something that he and his companions were not.

The provisions were loaded, but it was mid-afternoon before the party was finally ready to get going. The men were alarmed when they climbed into the vessels: There were only about four inches of freeboard. The load would lighten as they consumed food along the way, but in the meantime, they would have to be extremely careful; they would ship water easily if the river became rough. They pushed off from the shore, waving their paddles at the Indians who stood solemnly on the bank watching as the canoes slipped into the current like some beached sea creature returning home.

And what a grand treat those first few miles were compared to the long and arduous trek to Tete Jaune Cache. Now, the only effort required was to steer the canoes, for the river did all the work, sweeping them swiftly toward their destination. The banks flashed by and thrilled Will to a degree he had not experienced since he boarded the train back in London. They sped onward, rounding one bend after another with ease, but because of their late start managed only 20 miles for the day. Imagine if we had been underway for the entire day, Will thought. If these conditions continued, we could be at Fort George in a week!

The men allowed themselves a bit of a sleep-in the next morning, anticipating another day of easy drifting. The sun shone on the swirling river and the weather looked promising, but by late morning the sky darkened and the wind picked up. It blew into their faces so hard and with such a penetrating chill that they reluctantly pulled into shore at the first opportunity and made camp. With barely containable impatience, they sat in the tent listening to the wind moan through the trees. It blew into the evening and brought a driving rain that persisted throughout the night. They were startled awake in the morning by the tent collapsing on top of them, blown down by the wind that had grown to gale force. They took a straw vote about continuing despite the weather, and the consensus was that they could not afford to sit around for another day. They set out on the river once more, stroking hard, the water lapping dangerously close to the gunwales.

Paddling from the same position for too long caused their muscles to cramp, so they changed places frequently. Since this could not be done on the river for fear of swamping the canoes, it required pulling in to shore and became a time-consuming task that held them up. At least they were making headway in the face of the gale, even if it was slow, and they were grateful for that. It was not until well after lunch that the storm abated, and the wind dropped enough to allow the current to do most of the work again.

Farther downstream, it became apparent that the two canoes lashed together were too sluggish, and that they might make better time if they were separated. They grounded the vessels on the first sandy beach they came to and cut them apart. The Rennies took the large canoe while Helstone, Wright and Carpenter manned the smaller one.

The wind began blowing wildly again, across their bows on the tight bends in the river, and made it hard to steer. In the lead, the brothers rounded a rocky point and narrowly avoided a gravel bar, but Helstone, steering the second canoe, did not see it until Wright shouted a warning. Too late. The bow caught on the bar and swung the vessel broadside to the current, flipping it over. The three men and their cargo — two canvas-wrapped packs and a rifle — were tumbled into the river. The water was shallow but desperately cold as the men scrambled to retrieve the packs before they floated away. The rifle sank to the bottom and was easily retrieved. Meanwhile, the brothers had heard Wright's shout, saw what happened, gingerly executed a turn and paddled back to help.

The canoe was turned upright, bailed out and reloaded, and the party got underway again, the soaked men refusing to take the time to change into dry clothes. However, after a couple of hours they were so cold that they had to call it quits and shouted for the Rennies to pull in at the first decent landing spot. They wasted no time getting a sizeable, warming fire going to dry out their clothes and the rifle. Then they talked about the wisdom of having separated the canoes.

"What's the point of more speed if it only increases the risk of being dumped in the river?" Helstone argued. "The canoes might be slow when they're tied together, but at least they're a lot safer. We might not be so lucky next time, especially if we hit a rock in deep water."

Everyone agreed, particularly Will, who knew that luck had played a part in preventing him from hitting the gravel bar too. He had probably rounded the point a fraction wider than Helstone, nothing more. The canoes were lashed together again.

For the next day and a half, rain poured down into the river valley, sometimes so hard it limited visibility and hindered progress. The temperature only needed to drop a couple more degrees, Will reckoned, and they would have a huge snowfall on their hands. But instead, the weather began to improve and the sun burst through the clouds to warm them and boost their morale. All were in a happy frame of mind when they heard a roar of water in the distance.

They were not familiar with the sound but recognized it instantly. Rapids! And they were not prepared for them. They paddled furiously for shore but the unwieldy vessels were slow to turn. In the bow, Gilbert grabbed the long painter and leapt into the icy water. Thomas followed him. Their heavy clothes dragged them under, but both were near enough to shore that the water was barely up to their chests. They struggled to their feet on the boulder-strewn, slippery bottom, and Thomas dove for the rope and grabbed it too. For a split second, Will didn't think they'd be able to hold the heavy vessels, but fortune took pity on them. The canoes bumped up against a submerged rock near the entrance to the rapids. Will and Carpenter jumped in the river and swam to help the brothers. Between the four of them, they were able to pull the canoes to shore.

They had landed on a tiny beach beneath a steep bluff, an unwelcoming piece of real estate in what Will had already concluded was an inhospitable land. Since there was no place to pitch a tent and precious little wood for a fire anyway, they decided not to delay tackling the rapids. The sooner they were done with them the better.

Will volunteered to climb above the river to get a measure of what they had to face. He began the ascent with freezing hands and a trembling jaw, and ended in a sweat. He almost dreaded what he would see and hoped that whatever it was, their limited canoeing skills could handle it. They were apprentices, he realized, without the luxury of a journeyman around for guidance. But he was pleased with what he saw, a manageable stretch of white water that he thought could be easily negotiated. Their gear would have to be portaged, though, to give them more freeboard, so he walked along the bluff a short distance to make sure the river was accessible at the bottom of the canyon. If anything, the slope down was gentler than the one he had ascended.

Back on the beach he filled the others in. "The rapids don't look all that difficult," he said, "but I don't think we can take the canoes down loaded. There's not enough freeboard and they'll be too hard to steer lashed together. I think our best bet is to separate them and that way Gilbert and I can take the big one through first. If no one wants to take the small one through, we can come back and get it. In the meantime, the rest of you can portage our gear down. Once you get up the bluff, it's fairly easy going."

Thomas and Carpenter, however, were not about to be denied the adventure of shooting the rapids and volunteered to man the small canoe. This arrangement also suited Helstone and Wright, with their limited swimming abilities. They would begin moving the supplies to the bottom of the rapids, and once the canoes were safely through, Will and the others would come back to help.

Will and Gilbert climbed into the big canoe and paddled out far enough to avoid the submerged rock. The swift water of the rapids caught them and they tore into the chute among two-foot waves. It was an exhilarating ride and much easier than they had anticipated. It seemed only an instant before they were through to the calmer waters at the bottom of the canyon. Two minutes later, Thomas and Carpenter came bouncing down, grinning in exultation. After securing the canoes in a tiny cove adjacent to a good campsite, they got a blazing fire going and returned to help the others with the portage. Afterward, they spent the remainder of the day drying out their clothes and re-lashing the canoes together.

Sparks flitted skyward from the campfire as the men sat around it, listening to the crackling wood amid the steady din of whitewater tumbling out of the canyon and echoing off the stony walls. There was a good feeling among them, a strong sense of companionship and of great accomplishment. The river had placed a major obstacle in their path and they had conquered it. With any luck at all, that would be their most severe test between the Cache and Quesnellemouth, and the rest of their journey would be uninterrupted. It was a pleasant thought upon which to retire.

After supper, while the others were preparing for bed, Will climbed to a vantage point high above the river where he could watch the water plunge through the canyon, repeating the same pattern over and over again. He filled a pipe, pulled a match from his pouch, struck it on the bowl and put it to the tobacco, sucking in deeply, enjoying the familiarity of each small gesture. To the west, a red band traced the horizon where the cloud-hidden sun was setting. What a strange country this is, he thought, with its rushing rivers and crowding mountains that could squeeze the soul out of a man. Its grandeur on a sunny day was breathtaking, but when the clouds were down and it was raining or snowing, he could think of no place more sombre and intimidating. It isn't the Indians we need to fear, as Helstone believes; it's this land. And where were all the animals? Other than birds and the occasional rodent, they had not seen anything since they entered the mountains. He had not expected to see multitudes, but he thought that he would at least have an opportunity to bag a deer or two, perhaps even a bear. It was as if they too were intimidated by the land and had fled somewhere else.

The red band disappeared from the horizon and the chill of winter was in the air. It was now a month past the fall equinox, and the days were growing shorter, something they did much faster at this latitude than back home. Right now, the season sat on the cusp of winter and any day the temperature might dip below zero and stay that way until spring. There would be snow, too, and plenty of it. He suddenly felt anxious to be at the goldfields, fill his pockets and be gone. He could stay in this land forever and not feel comfortable in it, could never call it home. Only gold could provide a suitable reward for enduring it. He tapped out the dying embers from his pipe on the rock, descended to the campsite and joined the others in the tent. He went to sleep with high hopes of what the coming days would bring.

He awakened fast. He did not think he had heard anything; rather he had sensed something. Something that was moving quite near the camp. His companions were stirring so he put his fingers to his lips.

"There's something out there," he whispered.

Ever so slowly, he turned back the buffalo robe. Then he heard what he had sensed, an animal moving through the snow. A big one from the sound of it. When he peered out from the shelter, he could not believe his eyes. It was not a rescue party, but it was the next best thing: a deer, a small buck, but one that would do them nicely. He reached for his rifle, wishing that it was the Henry and not the old muzzleloader. With trembling hands, he loaded the powder, rammed in a bullet and placed a cap beneath the hammer. He raised the cold stock of the rifle to his cheek. He concentrated, trying to hold himself steady, but he could not stop swaying and quivering slightly. He sighted the deer, which was only 15 to 20 yards away, remembering with vivid clarity the last opportunity to bag one, when the shot had nearly missed. He did not want the same thing to happen here. He had to drop the animal in its tracks because neither he nor his companions were capable of going too far afield after it. He drew in a deep breath and held it. Squeeze the trigger, he told himself, don't pull it. Ever so slowly, he began applying pressure. The hammer tripped and fell on the cap. *Snap!* No explosion, just the sharp sound of a misfire. He removed the cap and put in another. It seemed to take forever. *Snap!* Another misfire. He began to shake badly and could feel perspiration breaking out on his forehead. He suddenly felt nauseous. There was one other weapon, another rifle, and he slowly put down his own weapon and motioned for someone to hand it to him. But the deer, alarmed by something, bounded off and disappeared. He could have cried. It was as if the animal had bolted with their lives.

The others were angry and he was disgusted enough with himself that he did not even attempt an excuse. He should have taken better care of his weapon, but he had been feeling so weak lately that it was sometimes hard to get moving.

The lack of food was wearing them all out. Over the past week, the sum of their diet was two ravens and two tiny pieces of beaver tail, which they had finished off last night. Despite his hunger, he had found the meat revolting and tried not to think of it as he choked it down. Yet that morsel of food, which was quickly digested, its nutrients absorbed into his body, was now the only thing between him and outright starvation. He had felt hunger before, when he had missed a couple of meals on the same day, but it was one thing to have an empty gut and know that food would soon be available; it was quite another when it was not. Then, the gnawing hunger becomes a constant reminder of the possibility of your own dying.

The following morning, they easily ran a small rapid and shipped only a bit of water. Farther down, Helstone spotted a small sack caught up on a snag and, curious, they pulled the canoes over to investigate. The sack contained huckleberries, swollen and spoiled from being in the water a long time. The men could only surmise that one of the advance parties must have been upset on this rapid or the previous one and lost it. In a way, there was some comfort in finding the flotsam: It meant that others had probably not been as successful as they had in negotiating the rapids. But even more important, as far as Will was concerned, it was yet another sign, besides the campsites they had seen, that other human beings had passed through this desolate country. He always found that thought reassuring.

They continued downriver, the water smooth and the passage easy. Gradually, the valley began to widen and the river slowed to a sluggish pace. For a change, the men had to paddle hard to make good headway. It began to rain again, and later in the afternoon, the rain turned into huge, sodden snowflakes, then into a blinding snowstorm. Visibility was so poor that they had no choice but to leave the river and set up camp. There was no dry wood about for a fire, so they crawled beneath their blankets in wet clothes, shivering, and tried to get some sleep.

It alternately rained and snowed throughout the night, the rain noisily pelting the canvas overhead, but when they awoke in the morning, it was snowing heavily and an inch or more lay on the ground. The flakes fell fat and wet and made the routine task of preparing for departure onerous. They paddled all day down the sluggish river, drifting slowly at lunchtime while they ate. In the afternoon, the snow became sleet and then rain. It was still bitterly cold and by six in the evening, they had had enough. They made camp at a site used by one of the parties preceding them, a large one judging by the size of it. There must have been animals, too, if the trampled underbrush nearby was any indication

As the next day was Sunday, the men stayed put. They spent the day drying their belongings and getting some warmth into their bones. Carpenter had a chance for some extra rest as he was still not feeling up to par. "A persistent ague," he said when Will inquired about his health. "It'll pass." But Will thought that the lawyer had become slightly morose since they had run the rapids and was spending a good deal of his idle time writing in his journal.

Back on the river the next morning the rain fell in sheets, and the men could barely see where they were going. In only a few minutes, they were soaked to the skin again. When Will suggested that they pull in to shore and separate the canoes so that they could make better time, no one argued. The river was slower and safe here, so it should not be a problem. Nevertheless, they would have to be vigilant.

Satisfied that they had picked up the pace, they paddled until dark. The weather improved markedly the following day, but the speed of the river increased as the mountains closed in on them again. In the afternoon, they heard a distant rumbling of water so commanding they worried that a waterfall rather than a rapid awaited them. They paddled in to shore and snubbed the canoes less than 50 yards from the entrance to a formidable-looking canyon.

It was a primeval place, dark and ominous. Glistening rock walls soared high above the river, and here and there stunted trees grew from clefts in the rock. The men climbed over boulders as cold and slippery as ice, then up through stunted trees and underbrush to a lookout from which they could study the river. Will estimated it to be somewhere between two and three hundred feet below them. The rapids were furious, much worse than the previous ones, and were in three stages. The first was the shortest but the most severe. It took two quick turns, and there was a boulder near the entrance around which it would be difficult, if not impossible, to maneuver the awkward canoes. The last two stages looked less forbidding and Will thought that they could be negotiated with any luck at all. The men agreed on a plan: They would let the canoes down through the first rapid by rope, to a small backwater, and then paddle them through the last two rapids, which were too long for the ropes. The supplies, of course, would have to be portaged.

It was more than apparent that this would not be an easy passage. These rapids were far more dangerous than the last ones, and the portage alone, which would require carrying the supplies up to at least the height of land the men were standing on, and then back down, would probably take the rest of the day if not longer. Furthermore, the canoes had become waterlogged from their time in the river and were extremely heavy. They would be a dead weight at the end of the rope and hard to hold on to. But there was little else they could do. There was no turning back from here.

Emptying the canoes, the men piled their goods on the shore and John Wright attached a long rope to one end of the smaller vessel. Helstone joined him and together they let the river take the vessel in its powerful grip. Meanwhile, Gilbert went over the portage route to the backwater, watching the passage of the canoe where he could. It scraped against the canyon wall at times, bounced over hidden boulders that threatened to capsize it, but made it all the way down without any damage and shipping too much water. Gilbert pulled the vessel onto the shore and untied the long line. The men above the rapid pulled it back.

The big canoe was much heavier than the smaller one and even less controllable. All five men got on the line to let it down and as soon as it hit whitewater, it turned turtle. The tremendous weight and the powerful current nearly tore the vessel from their grasp, and they needed every ounce of their strength to hang onto it. Slowly, hand over hand, they let out the rope until at last the canoe slid into the backwater beside the smaller one.

Gilbert could not turn the vessel upright by himself, but was able to secure it. The knot of the long line was under water, so he cut it, then went back to help the others with the first stage of the portage.

Two trips were required to carry the supplies to the height above the backwater. Then they climbed down with the paddles and joined Gilbert in the task of righting the big canoe and bailing it out. There was some talk about who would run the canoes down to the bottom of the rapids. Only two men could be in each canoe, as a third would reduce the freeboard too much. Jim Carpenter, despite his ill health, and Thomas were the first to volunteer for the task.

"Are you sure you're up to it?" Will asked the young lawyer.

Carpenter shrugged and grinned weakly. "There's nothing like a little danger to make a man forget how bad he feels."

Once again, both Wright and Helstone were unequipped for the job, so it fell to Will and Gilbert, both strong paddlers and swimmers. After some discussion, and reassurance from Carpenter that he would be all right, it was decided that he and Will would go first in the big canoe and Thomas and Gilbert would follow in the smaller one once they knew the first one had made it down safely. The four paddlers climbed to a rocky outcrop for a final look at their opponent.

They studied the river for several minutes, looking for paths of dark water that they could follow, and found enough to weave a plausible route. Whether they could maneuver the canoes along it was an entirely different matter. They returned to the water's edge, anxious about the task before them.

Will wanted to have something to eat in the event that he and Carpenter were separated from the others or perhaps even stranded for a while. He tore at some jerky, wolfing it down in his nervousness, but Carpenter was not hungry and wrote in his journal instead. Once he had finished, Will was eager to get moving. It was best not to think too long about what they had to do. He and Carpenter stripped off their boots and outer jackets and got into the big canoe. The lawyer looked calm, resigned to the challenge ahead, but Will was trembling with fear. He hoped that the others did not notice when they pushed them off. As the steersman, he turned the bow toward the narrow chute. His companions called "Good luck" and "God be with you" while the river took the heavy dugout in its mighty grasp and shot it forward, as if it weighed nothing at all.

The route the paddlers had planned through the canyon ran along green tongues split by boulders and often separated by short patches of whitewater. All they could do was hope that chance and some strong paddling would allow them to stay on the tongues, avoid the boulders and stay afloat through the rough patches. In an instant, they were in the maelstrom, and the thunder of the immense volume of water as it was squeezed between the walls of the canyon was stupendous. Will scarcely had time to think before a huge boulder, jutting up from the waves, loomed in front of them. Both men paddled frantically to avoid a collision. They wanted to pass to the right and succeeded, more by good luck than by good management, and they flew past at a dizzying speed and into a sharp bend. Only fierce paddling in the opposite direction prevented them from smashing into a black rock wall slick with water. Will was astonished by the fury of the water. They slammed into a broad whirlpool so hard it jarred his teeth. The bulky canoe was spun around once, as if it were no greater than a matchstick, and spat out on the far side with incredible velocity.

Fear gripped Will with such intensity that he became disoriented and the picture in his mind of the planned route vanished. Now they were truly at the mercy of the river. The waves seemed gigantic, and one smashed over them, half-filling the canoe with water. Its limited maneuverability was now completely gone, and Will knew the river had beaten them. The canoe slid onto a submerged rock and turned bottom up, throwing both men into the torrent. They narrowly missed being struck by the vessel, but they managed to grab hold of its slippery bottom, Will at the stern and Carpenter at the bow. Hanging on for dear life, they reached the bottom of the second rapid but could not escape the current, which pulled them into the third one. The vessel turned broadside, hit another submerged rock, and began tumbling gunwale over gunwale. Unable to hang on any longer, the two men let go and began swimming for their lives. The canoe disappeared behind a wall of water.

The turbulence sucked Will beneath the waves, down into a world of dark green, holding him there so long he feared he would never take another breath of air again, that this was where his earthly journey would end. He was thinking of his mother as he shot through the surface, gasping for air in water boiling to a frenzy, only to be sucked under once more. Again and again the river pulled him down, and each time he had less breath to hold. Just as he felt a dangerous lethargy overcoming his will to survive, he was out of the fury of the rapids and in calm but swiftly flowing waters. He looked around, but could not see Carpenter anywhere.

Exhausted, he turned on his back and floated, gasping for air like an asthmatic, trying desperately to fill his lungs. Water ballooned his shirt out and increased his weight until he felt perilously close to sinking. He yanked the tails out of his heavy wool pants, which helped some, but his body was so cold that he thought he might cramp up. He tried to swim to shore but his arms felt like useless sticks. He struggled, fully aware that he was in a fight for his life and that if he did not reach land soon he was doomed. Through sheer willpower, he made it to some rocks near the riverbank and tried to grab hold of them. They were slick as eels, and his hands were so numb from the frigid water that he could not hang on. He began drifting again, battling the lethargy that was now within a hair's breadth of overtaking him. Three-quarters of a mile downstream from the backwater, the current drove him against a small, pebbly beach that he was able to sink his hands into and stop. Slowly, he hauled himself ashore. Out of nowhere came the thought that he wished his father were alive so that he could thank him for insisting that he learn to swim. He got up on his feet, water cascading from him, shaking so hard he thought he could hear his bones rattle, but it was only his teeth. That fleeting thought was replaced by another that caused his heart to sink further: the realization that he had landed on the side of the river opposite to his companions. And, God forbid, Carpenter might have drowned.

After a few moments to collect himself, he looked up and down the riverbank for his companion but could see nothing, only the dark water, almost placid here, its boulder-strewn edges crowded by densely forested slopes. He felt as helpless as a child and wanted to cry, but it was important to hold himself together. He made his way back upstream over the rocks in stockinged feet, checking for Carpenter along the way, but he did not see him, and the river offered no clues. It took a half-hour to reach a point across from the backwater where the others waited. They waved, excited by his return, and Gilbert shouted, "Are you all right? Where's Jim?"

Will shouted back, "I'm all right. Have you not seen him?" And the answer he both feared and expected came echoing back, clear, even against the sound of the rapids, "No!"

"Can you come over in the canoe to get me?" he called.

He could see his companions conferring, heads shaking from side to side. "It's too dangerous!" Gilbert yelled back.

Will did not blame them. Now that he knew firsthand what the rapids were really like, he would not have made the trip either.

"I'll try to find a place downstream to cross!" he called, and waved. He had to move and get some warmth in his body.

He retraced his path over the rocks to the foot of the canyon, back to the beach on which he had landed. It looked safe enough here to cross, but the cold dark water was daunting. He feared going back into it, but he had little choice in the matter. He would need to build more body heat before attempting to cross, though, so he ran around in circles, beating his chest with his arms. Once he felt warm enough, he considered stripping down to his underwear so that swimming would be easier, but then thought better of it. He would need his clothes and was not sure about being able to retrieve them. Fully clad, he waded into the river and struck out for the far shore, swimming as fast as he could. Halfway across, the cold nearly paralyzed him and the other side looked miles away. Panic seized him and he thrashed his way through the water with arms and legs that seemed to have lost all feeling. He was whimpering but did not care. God, he thought, I'll never make it. But he kept thrashing and choking on water, tearing a pathway across the river until at last his numb hands touched solid ground. Sobbing with relief, he crawled up the bank like some creature from another era, and lay there gasping for breath. When he found the strength to move, he dragged himself to his feet, shivering uncontrollably, then staggered back upstream to join the others, wondering if the cold would finish him off, complete what the river had failed to do.

"Did you see Carpenter?" his companions asked when he reached them. It was a question riddled with anxiety, and Will wished he had some good news to tell them. He shook his head. "He's gone," he said, fighting back tears. He dug out his only change of clothing from his pack and dressed, his teeth rattling all the while. Gilbert got a blanket and placed it around his shoulders.

The others looked as troubled as Will felt. They had not foreseen this, had refused to think that such a horrible thing could happen, and were now in a quandary over what to do. Yet, despite their confusion, one thing was clear: They could not stay here. If they could get the small canoe through the rapids, then some could ride in it while others walked, and they could spell each other off. If need be, they could all climb in to get around impassable points of land, or make two trips. That was only possible, however, if they were able to get the vessel to the bottom of the canyon. No one was willing to put himself at risk by taking it down, least of all Will, who would have argued vehemently against such foolishness anyway. The best they could come up with was to set it adrift and hope it could find its own way down. Before they did that though, they would portage the supplies down to where Will had landed. Gilbert would then swim across the river with one end of a rope and secure it upstream from the other end. When the canoe came down, it would hit the rope and follow the diagonal into shore, where it could be easily retrieved. If that failed, they would divide the provisions up in their packs and start walking. They estimated that Fort George could be as far as 200 miles away, but with any luck at all they might be able to reach it in 8 to 10 days.

Will packed the blanket and threw a coil of rope over his shoulder while the others loaded up with goods and began the trek downstream. He felt better moving, doing something constructive. Across from the pebbly beach, Gilbert stripped and, tying one end of the rope around his waist, plunged into the frigid river and swam as fast as he could to the far shore. There was a fallen tree with a thick limb sticking into the water, and he tied the rope there, as close to the surface as possible. They could not have it too high, because a completely submerged canoe would pass beneath it. Will did the same thing at his end, about 10 yards downstream, and left some slack in the rope so that it sagged into the river. It was by no means foolproof, but it was the best they could do, and if worst came to worst, one of the brothers would jump in after it. Gilbert found the clothes that Will had shed and gathered them up — they were much too valuable to leave behind — then splashed into the river and used the rope to pull himself back to the others.

They all headed up to the backwater for the rest of their gear. Once there, Helstone volunteered to stay behind, and when he figured everyone was back at the rope, he would push the canoe into the rapids and hope the river would do the rest. He waited for as long as it had taken them to make the first trip down, plus 10 minutes more. Then he waded into the water and gave the canoe a good shove. It floated out toward the rapids where a small eddy caught it and would not let go. He groaned aloud. Damn it! What else could go wrong? He threw rocks at the canoe but it would not budge and circled lazily in the eddy. With little else to be done, he headed downriver to relay the bad news.

Meanwhile, the others had arrived at the beach and were waiting for the canoe to come down. Ten minutes passed, then fifteen. A half hour slipped by and still no canoe. They waited, impatiently, wondering what had happened to Helstone, when they saw him appear from behind some rocks on the riverbank, an exasperated look on his face.

"The damned thing is caught in an eddy!" he said. "I pushed it as hard as I could."

"Damn it!" said Will. His inclination was to blame Helstone for a job improperly done, and he was sure that the others were thinking the same thing, but he resisted. The canoes were awkward objects to move and this was no time to start an argument. They all needed each other. He said only, "Maybe it'll rain enough overnight to raise the water level a bit so that it'll come down by itself."

Daylight was almost gone as they set up camp, unable to believe their run of bad luck.

Will found himself glancing upriver every few minutes in hopes that he would spot the canoe drifting down. The thought of walking to Fort George this late in the season made his stomach hurt. It could prove to be a desperate journey at best.

Later that evening they were going through Carpenter's belongings and everyone was in a sombre mood. Will found the young lawyer's journal. At first he was reluctant to open it, but then decided that perhaps it contained his home address. When they reached safety, they would need to inform his wife of his passing. He found an address at the very front of the leather-bound book, yet could not resist thumbing through some of the entries. Most chronicled the lawyer's daily activities and some were small love notes and poems to his wife. Will gasped when he read the last entry. A single sentence on a page all by itself, it read: "Arrived this day at the canyon at 10 A.M. and drowned running the canoe down; God keep my poor wife."

Chapter Six

October 1862

Will was first up the next morning and stuck his head out of the tent to see if the canoe had come down. It had not. There had been rain during the night but not enough to dislodge the vessel or the rope had failed to trap it.

He and the others had not yet recovered emotionally from the previous day's events. Carpenter's death was devastating, and they mourned his loss. Will trembled at the thought of how close he had come to joining the lawyer, and during a restless night had wondered why he had survived and Carpenter had not. It might have been that the young man was weak from his illness and could not fight the river or, in predicting his death, he had just given up. It might also have been something as simple as their positions in the canoe and the ends they were hanging onto when the vessel turned broadside. Carpenter may have collided with a rock that knocked him senseless. Whatever had happened, he was gone, and Will wished he could turn the clock back to Fort Edmonton, when Carpenter had asked to join them, and give him back his life by saying no. He had spoken of his feelings last night in the intimacy of the tent, and Gilbert gripped his arm and said, "It's a great tragedy, Will, there's no denying it. But we almost lost you and that would have been worse."

"How could that have been worse? Is my life worth more than his?"

"I didn't mean that. I meant it would have been worse for Thomas and me. Especially for Mother."

Will said nothing. He did not relish the days ahead of them. The circumstances could only be more critical if they had lost their entire food supply as well. As it was, they could only pack what they could carry and would need to shoot an animal or two to survive. The men agreed that someone should run up to the backwater to see if the canoe was still there. Thomas quickly volunteered and returned with the news that it was gone.

So it had indeed come down during the night and had slipped by their trap. Now it was somewhere downriver, but how far was anybody's guess. It might conceivably float all the way to the coast.

The men sorted out their belongings, taking only those things they could carry on their backs: blankets, food, cooking utensils, an extra change of clothing each and, among them, two machetes and two rifles. They would also take the rope stretched across the river. The rest they cached, rolled up in the tent, just in case they found the big canoe farther downstream and could come back for it. Gilbert swam the river for the rope, tied it around his waist, and was hauled back like a big fish.

They fought their way along the torturous riverbank, over fallen trees and rocks, until they came to a place where a granite shoulder dropped straight into the river. The only way around it was to climb the steep slope beside them. They clawed their way to the top, using a machete to slash their way through walls of thick underbrush. They were a hundred feet or more above the river before the slope flattened out. The forest was dense up here, and a man would not have to be too far in it to be lost forever. It was important to keep the river in sight at all times, or at least the open space above the river, here on high ground. It was their lifeline to Fort George, and if they strayed from it and could not find their way back, they were probably as good as dead. They wove a path through the trees along the edge of the high bluff and came to a steep gully. They worked their way down to the bottom, over boulders and small rocky ledges, through scrub brush, hanging onto branches and small fallen trees on the way. It was tricky and dangerous in spots, and they moved slowly, keenly aware of the consequences of breaking an arm or a leg. Reaching the bottom, they shed their packs and rested their quivering leg muscles while Thomas followed the gully to the river to see if the shoreline was passable. It wasn't. They donned their packs and scaled the far side over similar terrain, equally steep, and despite the chill air, they were sweating profusely by the time they reached the top. From there, the land was relatively level, but the forest was strewn with deadfall and boulders. It did not seem as if they had gone very far before they came upon another deep gully.

"Good God!" Thomas said. "We'll never make Fort George if the trail's going to be like this! We'll run out of food before we're 50 miles downriver."

"It has to change," Will said. "It can't stay like this forever." But that wasn't what he thought. He was gloomy enough to believe that it might indeed go on forever, maybe even beyond in this cursed country.

The descent to the bottom of the second gully proved even more treacherous than the first. On the bottom they shed their packs again for a rest before climbing out and went to the river for a drink. They argued later about who spotted it first, but there, across the river, was the big canoe, half-filled with water yet still upright, caught in a snarl of small trees and branches that almost hid it. Gilbert claimed that he saw it first but thought he was hallucinating. Jubilant cries from the others confirmed that he was not. What an incredible stroke of luck! They could all fit in the big one. It would be tight and precarious, no doubt about that, but they would make it work somehow. First, though, they had to get across the river to retrieve it.

Though they desperately needed the vessel, there was not much enthusiasm about swimming the river. Even Gilbert, who prided himself on being a strong swimmer, did not think he could make the distance in water so cold. But he had an idea. They would chop down three scrub spruces with trunks about eight inches in diameter, then trim them and lash them together. This would make a small raft that they could straddle and, using a couple of thick limbs, paddle over to the canoe. They would probably be mostly under water during the crossing, but they would not have to swim and they could leave their clothes on for warmth. He was certain that he and Will could do it.

With energy renewed by the prospect of success, they quickly felled the trees, trimmed the branches, then dragged the logs to the river's edge and lashed them together. It was a crude affair, but it floated and that was all they wanted. The brothers hung their metal drinking cups, which they would use for bailing, on twine around their necks and climbed aboard. They sank up to their buttocks in the water but no lower, and eased into the current, pleased with the stability of their creation. Had the circumstances not been so serious it might have been funny, because to those on shore it looked as if the brothers had nothing beneath them as they stroked their invisible craft to the far side. When they reached the canoe, an even bigger surprise awaited them. There, upside down and completely submerged, but also caught by the snag, was the smaller canoe. The brothers waved their paddles in triumph. "The other canoe's here too!" Will shouted, and he could hear his companions whooping in delight over the amazing news.

The brothers' legs were going numb, but their elation made it tolerable. They bailed as fast as their small cups would allow, scooping the water in one continuous motion from the dugout back into the river. It was a slow and arduous process, but they were soon scraping the bottom. They climbed in and, removing the ropes from their makeshift raft, let the logs drift off. Since the small canoe was not going anywhere, they left it for a couple of the others to retrieve and paddled victoriously back to them.

Wright and Thomas could barely restrain themselves from getting into the canoe before Will and Gilbert got out. They were gone in a flash for the other side, while the brothers shed their wet clothes and warmed up by the fire that Helstone had had the good sense to build. They watched as the other vessel was righted and bailed, watched as both canoes were paddled back, and were delighted as much with themselves as they were with the turn of events.

They had tea and a pipe and then drew twigs, like straws, to decide who would paddle back upriver to bring down the rest of their goods. Gilbert, Thomas and Helstone won the honour and were back before nightfall. They had looked for Carpenter, both on the way up and on the way down, but had not seen him. Helstone guessed that after he drowned and sank beneath the surface, his body was probably caught on a snag.

The men set up a proper camp, pleased that they would be inside a tent for the night, and had extra portions of smoked salmon to celebrate their victory over tremendous odds. The intense feelings of camaraderie had returned since they had survived yet another ordeal, and they chatted like schoolchildren. True, they had only managed a couple of miles today, but all were convinced that the river had shown the last of its troublesome side and would now convey them swiftly to Fort George. Today's events were a good omen, if ever there was one. They carved some proper paddles before turning in.

He had stopped counting the days. The effort was too painful, both physically and mentally. The last notch he had made was the 18th and that must have been nearly a week ago. He had also stopped going to the river with the spyglass. There was too much disappointment in it.

Their clothes hung on them like the rags that they had become and their faces were gaunt behind unruly beards. All of them had lost an alarming amount of weight, and they were spending more time beneath their buffalo robes. Now they could only hope that another animal would wander into camp. The thought of what would happen if none did was too dreadful to contemplate. On fair-weather days they were taunted almost daily by birds that flew high overhead, and they occasionally heard a raven's hoarse *corruk* but they could rarely get their weapons ready fast enough to do anything about it. When they talked, food was often their favourite topic, and they would concoct imaginary meals of enormous sustenance, mostly poor recollections of recipes that their wives and mothers had cooked for them. He even fantasized about the soup they would have been able to make had all or part of the moosehide rope been left behind. There were moments when he would have given anything just to chew on a piece of it. The only thing in their surroundings that they recognized as edible was rosehips, from which they made tea before devouring them. But the bushes were depleted and they were down to the last few that they had collected. One night he broached a subject that, thus far, no one had dared talk about.

"Do you know what I've been thinking?" He was picking at a rosehip with his teeth, bit by bit, savouring and chewing each nibble as if he were eating an apple. His chin was on his chest and he did not look up. "Do you know the story of the Donner party?"

His companions knew vaguely of it.

"The Donners were part of an overland expedition from the eastern United States," he told them, "who tried to reach California by wagon train in 1846. This was before the big gold rush, so they were heading out there to make a new life for themselves. Wagonloads of families — men, women and children with as much experience as we had. Just like us, they also didn't think it would take long to reach their destination. Then, like the damned fools they were, they tried a new route through the desert because they thought it would be shorter. It was shorter, all right — a shorter trip to eternity for a lot of them. By the time they reached the Sierra mountains, winter had set in hard and fast and trapped them before they knew it. One by one, some of the older people began dying off, and it didn't take long for the rest to figure out what to do with the bodies. They used them for food. Ate them. Cannibals, they were."

In the morning, they lashed the canoes together and set out on the river with light hearts. The current, though not dangerous, was brisk enough that they only had to steer. The mountains had disappeared among the clouds again and a mist hung above the water that, combined with the moss-laden trees lining the banks, gave the river an eerie quality. It stayed that way for most of the morning, and Will felt like a character in one of the old fables his mother used to read to him. Nonetheless, the river was at least friendly and offered up no surprises.

They were making good time, paddling only when there was a need to warm up. They did not stop for lunch, so intent were they on making progress, and instead snacked on some smoked salmon in the canoe. A cold rain came and went, but it did not matter as much now that their optimism had returned. Their high spirits received an even bigger boost when Helstone shot two ducks and a couple of squirrels to add to the larder.

That night in camp, they plucked the ducks and skinned and gutted the squirrels. They split all four carcasses open, spread them apart, and skewered them with sharpened sticks across the undersides to hold them open. Then they shoved longer sticks beneath the crosspieces and propped them up by rocks over the fire. Fat dripping from the roasting meat sizzled and burned and sent up plumes of dark smoke. The smell was exquisite, and when the meat had nearly blackened, the men ate it, picking every bone bare and licking their fingers clean of grease. They had not had such a scrumptious meal since Tete Jaune Cache, which now seemed so long ago, the pleasure was hard to remember.

They were away with the dawn and spent another good day on the river but awoke the following morning to a violent snowstorm. They would rather have stayed put when forward visibility was so limited and the weather so miserable, but the consensus was that they had to keep moving. Fort George could not be far away, and they would be all right as long as the river stayed as benign as it had been the past three days.

By mid-afternoon, the storm had abated and the clouds lifted. Under different circumstances, Will thought, the scene before them would be quite beautiful: snow-draped trees against a misty backdrop, the hard angles of black boulders along the shore softened by contours of white, and the river itself, bending peacefully in the foreground. He hoped that the storm was not a precursor to even more snow and colder weather. If the river started to freeze, they would really find a peck of trouble.

The double canoe glided along almost effortlessly, the combination of paddle and current working together to eat up the miles. They passed through a long, wide canyon and continued on in an easy rhythm, lulled by the repetition of scenery and movement. Then a strange sound came to them across the misty water that at first they did not recognize. It was an anomaly in this savage wilderness. The sound came again, and then they knew what it was: the voices of children at play.

They did not understand the language and knew that it had to be Indians. Rounding a bend in the river, they saw two canoes pulled up on the bank in front of an encampment. Would the inhabitants be as friendly and helpful as the Shuswap had been back at the Cache? There was only one way to find out. They steered toward shore.

Two small children, bundled up against the cold, with red cheeks and runny noses reacted like startled deer when they saw the five white men gliding closer in their massive dugouts. They spun in their tracks and took refuge inside a crude log house with a bark roof. Three native women came out, wearing heavy wool dresses that were obviously European. One of the women was old, her face a network of creases, and wore a small leather pack on her back. Will guessed that she was probably the matriarch. He had never seen more filthy human beings and wondered if they kept themselves that way as a means of protection from the elements. They looked both defiant and frightened, for there seemed to be no men around. Will presumed that the husbands were away hunting. Recognizing that communication was going to be a challenge, he instructed the others to smile to let the women know that they were friendly and did not intend any harm. They beached their canoes beside the Indian vessels and went ashore.

The camp included the dwelling, a fire pit with some drying racks in front and, to the side propped up against a tree, a wood frame over which a moosehide was stretched taut for scraping.

"It's a small camp," Helstone said to no one in particular. "That means fewer savages." Will knew that Helstone still did not trust Indians, despite the positive nature of his previous encounters with them, and was probably feeling grateful for the good news.

Still smiling, the men nodded their heads and said hello. The women made no reply of any kind and only stared harder at the intruders. Will reckoned that if the Indians had any food to trade, it might be a good idea to supplement their own provisions just in case they experienced more delays downriver. He made circular motions over his belly with his hand and pretended to eat but the women responded only by shaking their heads. Just then, two Indian men, dressed in filthy leggings and animal-skin robes, appeared from out of the forest. Long, greasy hair hung out from under European toque-like hats. Both men had ancient rifles, carried so they were ready to use at only a moment's notice. They eyed the visitors with suspicion. Will held up his hand in greeting, even more nervous now, and was surprised when one of the men responded in pidgin. Where had he learned his English, Will wondered. Then it dawned on him. He must have picked it up from white men at the fort. His heart jumped. The fort! It could not be very far away then.

"How far is it to Fort George?" he asked, pointing down the river, and was crestfallen when the Indian said it was a four- or five-day paddle. Yet when he thought about it, he did not quite believe it. They had been on the river too long and had come too many miles for it to be true. He reckoned they were no more than two days away from the fort, at the most, and that the Indian was exaggerating in order to strengthen his bargaining position should the white men want anything. Will asked if they had any food to trade, but the Indian merely shrugged and said that many other white men had passed this way over the past couple of months, some on monstrous rafts the likes of which the Indians had never seen before, and had needed food. Now their supplies were low, which was one of the reasons they were hunting.

In the end, Will and the others traded most of Carpenter's clothes for some dried beaver tails and moose meat that included some fat, and felt that they had come out on the short end of the stick. There was nothing they could do about it, however, as they were not in any position to demand more. On the positive side, they had extra food now, which should see them nicely through to Fort George.

The Indians invited the men to pitch their tent next to the dwelling, but after a brief discussion out of earshot, they decided that it might be wiser not to. Will had no strong feelings about it either way, but there was a general mistrust of the Indians among the others, mostly instigated by Helstone, who said, "We'd have to guard our things all night, otherwise they'll be rob us blind. We'll get a better night's sleep downriver."

Will agreed that caution was probably the best course of action. If they were robbed, it would only serve to place them in jeopardy once again and they had had more than their fill of that. They thanked the Indians for the generous offer, stowed the meat in the canoes and took their leave.

They travelled only a few miles before darkness forced them in to shore to make camp. Will believed that they were far enough away from the Indians to be safe but Helstone disagreed, insisting that they set up an armed watch throughout the night. "Two hours each should get us through to morning," he said. "And those not on watch will sleep a lot easier." Will thought Helstone was being overly cautious, but as everyone else seemed to agree, he went along with them.

A fire was kept going all night and water on the boil for tea. Will took the watch at two o'clock, relieving John Wright. He came out of the tent just as the clouds began pulling back to reveal a silent symphony of stars. The clouds had been crowding the mountains for so long that it was a welcome sight. He got himself into a comfortable position to gaze heavenward, listening for paddle sounds from the river gurgling by, not believing for a moment that he would actually hear the Indians if they came. He thought about Fort George and was excited about being so near to it. They still had a hundred miles or so to go beyond the fort to see the last of this river for a while, but the fort represented civilization and they could all use a little of that. It was two months since they had left Fort Edmonton and danced with those pretty girls. The thought aroused him and he wondered what delights Fort George would have to offer.

He had been watching the stars for several minutes when he was thunderstruck by a revelation: the North Star was aligned with the direction of flow of the river. Since the river had been running relatively straight, it meant that they had at last turned south and were nearing Fort George. After they passed through a long canyon, Will had felt certain that the river was swinging southward in a giant arc, but persistently low clouds prevented getting a proper bearing. Now he had solid proof that they were closing in on the fort, and the map supported it. He estimated two days of paddling to get there, maybe less. It was a thrilling discovery that made the rest of his watch pass slowly, because he could not wait to tell Thomas, who would be up next.

The morning was cold but the sky was clear for a change and the men, spurred on by the good news, were back on the river before full light. By mid-morning the wind began to pick up and by noon was blowing so furiously that it churned the placid river into a heavy sea against which they could make no headway whatsoever. All they could do was retreat to the shore and wait out the storm, impatient to get moving again. But it blew a gale right through the evening and into the early morning.

There was still a severe chop on the water when they awoke, and if they had had a choice, they would have stayed in the tent. But they could not delay any longer. Each day was colder than the previous one, and they knew that if it had not been for the wind, ice would be forming in the still backwaters, and it would not be long before the river was too frozen for travel.

It was dangerous on the river. Some parts of it were exposed to the wind more than others, particularly where a bend was broad, and in these places, the waves threatened to swamp them. Twice they were frightened out of their wits when a huge wave splashed over the gunwales, forcing them to bail furiously to keep from sinking. But they persevered and paddled on with caution, every dip of the paddles a victory, and by early evening the wind had subsided and the river was placid once more. They scarcely had time to relax when they heard the noise that they had all come to dread: the sound of smooth water being broken up over rocks. More rapids. Without a word said among them, they stroked for the shore.

It was hard to get the measure of these rapids, because there was not a decent height of land from which to study them. Will and John Wright scouted downriver only a short distance, for it was rough going, but from what they could see, the rapids were not that severe and the canoes should run them easily, even tied together. There were boulders jutting up here and there, and places where it was obvious that the water was passing over submerged ones, but other than that, they ought to be able make the passage without too many problems, as long as they were careful. They would also have to be vigilant in the event the rapids worsened.

It was late afternoon, and the men discussed whether they should try to run the rapids now or wait until morning.

"Let's do it now," Helstone said, before anyone else could contribute their thoughts, "and get this damned trip over and done with. I don't know about the rest of you, but I've about had enough."

That summed up everyone else's feelings: they all wanted to see the end of it. By running the rapids now, they might reach Fort George as soon as tomorrow, which was incentive enough for anyone harbouring traces of doubt. They climbed back in the canoes and pointed them downriver.

The entrance to the rapids was wide, probably a hundred yards or more. The men figured they would stand a better chance in the middle, even though they feared being so far away from shore. In any event, that was where they steered the canoes. Will's heart was in his throat as they entered the choppy water. He could feel the canoes surge forward as they picked up speed and guessed that the current was probably running 10 miles an hour or more. At that speed, the canoes were moving fast enough that the men would be hard-pressed to avoid anything dangerous. The two bowmen were the lookouts, one short range, the other long. It was imperative that they keep alert for any signs that the river was changing for the worse.

It was hard and tricky work trying to avoid the occasional boulder in their path; more than once the bulky vessels scraped against solid rock and threatened to turn broadside. The current seemed to be carrying them closer to the west bank where there were more rocks to contend with, but there was little they could do about it. The river was the master here.

Despite his apprehension, Will found the ride exhilarating and he felt as if they were in complete control of the situation, that they had acquired enough skills over the past two weeks to handle the capriciousness of these intricate waters. Then, in an attempt to avoid a submerged rock over which the water rose before dipping and curling into a sizeable wave, they swung broadside to the current. The men struggled to straighten the vessel out, but it rose up on yet another submerged boulder and came to a grinding halt.

Chapter Seven

October 1862

The collision nearly threw the men out of the canoes, which now sat at a slight tilt on the rock. At the low end, the small one was shipping water as the river surged around it, sending Helstone and Wright scrambling into the large one. Their departure raised the gunwale enough to keep the vessel above the river, but the canvas-wrapped packs sat in several inches of water.

Will cursed in utter disbelief. "Let's see if we can rock this bloody thing off!" he said, half-shouting to be heard over the rush of the water. The others were more angry than frightened as they grasped the gunwales to try to dislodge the canoes. They shifted their weight around from one canoe to the other and from one end to the other, and even tried paddling them off, but their efforts failed to budge the vessels. They were stuck fast.

"What do we do now?" Wright asked, fear apparent in the question.

"Maybe we should pray," said Helstone, only half-joking.

"You might be right," Will said. "But for now, I think we should just wait and see what this bloody river does. It looks like it could rain and maybe it'll rise. If not, we'll have to separate the canoes.

We should be able to get the small one off and get two or three of us to shore. Then we can throw a rope out and try to pull this one off."

"Let's do it now," said Thomas.

"No. It's too risky, and there's not much daylight left if something goes wrong."

So they waited, impatiently and silently, each man lost in his thoughts. Daylight dwindled fast beneath the leaden skies and the descending darkness pressed down on the men, saturating them with despair. Will felt full of nervous energy for which there was no outlet. He did not relish spending a night on this tiny, unnatural island in the middle of these churning waters, but was satisfied with the wisdom of his opinions. They dug out some of the dried moose meat that the Indians had traded them and had supper. Afterward, they wrapped themselves in their blankets to await the dawn, all too aware that a long night loomed ahead.

The falling darkness soon enveloped them as utterly as their gloom. Snow fell heavily out of the night. Will tried talking to Gilbert, who was closest to him, but his brother's spirit had sunk to a low ebb and he was monosyllabic. The attempt to converse, like the canoes, became stuck on its own rock. Since talking in a normal voice was difficult with the river rushing around them, the men remained isolated from one another. Had it been possible to read their minds, a single thought might have been prevalent among them, repeated many times over: "What on Earth are we doing here?"

Will was still dumbfounded over what had happened. It seemed as if some invisible force was determined to thwart their passage to the goldfields or, at the very least, lay down serious obstacles so that they might better appreciate the gold should they be lucky enough to find any. He believed a man made his own fate, but times like these seemed bent on proving him wrong: that instead of being the captain of his fate, he was merely a foot soldier slogging through an endless series of events over which he had no control.

The river surged and hissed all around them and he tried to ignore the noise. It was downright frightening to be stuck on a rock in the dark on a wild river, in a wild land, one of those things that could easily get the best of a man if he let it. He could not get fully warm or comfortable in the cramped space that was his, and sleep was elusive. If the constant shifting around by the others was any indication, they were having a tough time of it, too. Expletives cut through the sound of the river. He tried to think positive thoughts and fantasized about hearth and home and warming drinks of rum and eggnog, those colourful women, as the snow fell even thicker and formed a white wall mere feet from his eyes. It settled on the men and their belongings and turned them into unrecognizable mounds that from the shore would have looked like any other irregularly shaped rocks jutting up from the river. But unlike rocks, they felt the piercing cold.

Will had no idea what time it was when he finally dozed off from sheer exhaustion, but it seemed only moments before a loud thump of something hitting the canoes startled him awake. The others jumped too, alarmed by the noise. The snow had stopped and Will peered upriver into the night just as a sizeable chunk of ice came out of the darkness and thudded into the small canoe, scraped along its side, then moved off with the current. He groaned inwardly. As if they did not have enough problems, the river was freezing up. But when he thought about it, maybe a strike by a big enough chunk of ice would dislodge them. If not, they had better get off this rock at first light, and be quick about it. He dared not think of the consequences if they failed.

The men scarcely slept at all the rest of the frigid night. They would just nod off when another block of ice would hit the canoes and jolt them awake. First light plodded toward them as slow as an arthritic old man. When it arrived at last, the first thing Will noticed was that the level of river had had dropped even further, heralding more bad news. Much more and their circumstances would dramatically shift from the difficult to the impossible.

They ate some jerky for breakfast and tried, with small movements, to work some warmth back into their blood and some flexibility into their limbs. Will had never seen a group of men look so grim, and he doubted that he looked any better. After a brief discussion as to how best to go about it, they got busy with the task of trying to free themselves.

Since the smaller canoe was not as firmly lodged on the rock as the large one, they decided to separate them. They would load the smaller vessel with as many supplies as possible, and three men would try to get it to shore. Two paddlers, they reasoned, might not be enough to control the vessel in the swift current. It was a tricky business confronting them, because they would have to cut the lashings before anyone got in, at which point the canoe would be seriously unstable. On the other hand, if they all got in before the separation, it would be so heavy that it probably would not go anywhere. Once they got to shore, regardless of whether or not they were able to pull the large canoe off, they would at least be able to light a fire, something they needed badly. As for getting the remaining two men ashore, they would deal with that when the time came.

It was agreed that Will, Helstone and Wright would man the small canoe. There was considerable risk to this venture for Helstone and Wright, because of their lack of swimming skills. If the canoe tipped over and spilled them into the river, there was a chance they would not survive. But everyone felt it was best to leave two swimmers behind. It would be less traumatic for them if they had to come across by rope.

They opened up some of the packs and, using the tent, made a special casing for some food, cooking utensils and a rifle. They secured it with the remainder of the rope. Meanwhile, Gilbert had bailed out the small canoe and after the pack was transferred, the three men prepared to leap in. Gilbert and Thomas quickly slashed the connecting ropes and grabbed the gunwales of the smaller vessel while the others jumped in. The canoe came dangerously close to capsizing when the river took it in its awesome grasp. Then, just as it began to move away from the rock, just when they thought they had made it, a huge piece of ice crashed into the vessel's side and flipped it over.

All three men hurled themselves at the main canoe. Will and Helstone managed to catch the gunwales, but Wright missed by inches and the powerful current swept him away, screaming for help. Will's body was nearly horizontal, half in and half out of the water. He could feel the rock beneath him and tried to scramble up on it but it was too slippery. The water was numbing and he felt the tremendous pull of the river, exacerbated by the weight of his waterlogged clothes. Fear was the glue that kept him from losing his grip. He felt Thomas grab his arms, wondered where his brother would find the strength to lift him, but felt his feet drag over the rock, his body scrape over the gunwales of the canoe, and then he thudded onto the bottom, safe from the awful river. He rolled onto his back, fighting to fill his lungs with air, and accidentally kicked Helstone, who had been hauled into the vessel by Gilbert. "Thank you, Thomas," Will said, when he was finally able to catch a breath, stuttering from the terrible cold. "I couldn't have made it without you."

The four men had been so busy with their own predicament that they had not seen what happened to Wright. They knew that he had disappeared, but could not say whether it was beneath the water or around the first bend in the river. Will and Helstone stripped off their pants and underwear and wrung them out, shivering all the while, then wrapped themselves in the buffalo robes to get warm. Will was exasperated by their string of bad luck and cursed himself as a bloody fool for being on this river. They had lost Carpenter and now Wright was gone, and they were still stranded on a rock in an unforgiving river, with no foreseeable way of getting off. Will's mood turned black with despair, and the fear that seared his soul was unlike anything he had felt before.

Thomas was near tears and furious. He and Wright had gotten closer over the months of travel despite the differences in their personalities and ambitions. "He should never have been here," he said. "He was a homebody, a family man. He shouldn't have come."

"It's my fault," Helstone said. "I made him come. Now he's gone."

Helstone's admission of fault surprised Will. The man rarely acknowledged that he was wrong about anything. But was Wright really gone? Will believed that he was. How could anyone survive in the turmoil of that glacial water, especially a non-swimmer? It seemed to Will that it was even colder than it had been back at the canyon, as near to ice as it could get without actually being frozen solid. He looked at Helstone. "Maybe the trip was jinxed, doomed to fail from the start," He offered this as consolation but felt despondent enough to believe it. "Anyway, there's no point in laying blame. It won't get us anywhere. If anyone's got any good suggestions, though, let's hear them."

But there were no brilliant ideas forthcoming that might cast even the smallest glimmer of light into the pall of gloom that enshrouded their lives. The men lapsed into silence, the only sounds the mad swirl of the river and the occasional thump of ice striking the canoe.

They remained that way for a long time. Then Gilbert saw something moving along the shore. At first, he thought it might be a deer or a bear. Then it took on a human form. "It's Johnny!" he shouted. Will looked and sure enough, there was Wright, slowly making his way along the riverbank toward them. The men were ecstatic, Helstone especially, and simultaneously let out a loud cheer that Wright heard. He waved at them. Will believed in miracles.

His companions were appalled by the Donner story, but he plowed on. "The odd thing is that when most people heard about it, they said they would rather die than eat another human being. The mere thought of it horrified them, they said, and maybe so. But there's an unspoken agreement among shipwrecked seamen that eating the dead is quite an acceptable means of survival. It's happened often enough that the practice is considered a custom of the sea, and when you think about it, it makes sense. Accusations of depravity only come from the well-fed. Besides, the law has never looked too harshly upon those who've had to resort to it."

His companions looked at each other as if they suspected him of preparing them for the unthinkable. Maybe he was. Or maybe he was paving a path to the inevitable.

"That won't happen to us," one said. "Help will come.
It has to." But help was not coming, and the sooner
they all resigned themselves to that fact, the better. The
idea of eating the two men who sat beside him, or them
eating him, was not something he wished for, but when
the time came, if one of them died before him, he would
be mentally prepared.

He said, "I think it's about time we all faced up to
the reality of our situation. We've been here more than
a month now and you know as well as I do what the
weather's been like. Do you think it's any better 5, 10 or
20 miles downriver, or however far they may have got?
Wake up! No one's coming."

When Wright reached a spot across from the stranded men,
Will cupped his hands around his mouth and yelled, "Are you all
right?"

Wright called back, "I'm freezing. Can you throw me some
matches and an axe? I need to get a fire going."

While Helstone wrapped some matches in a small piece of
oilskin and tied the bundle to the handle of a hatchet, Wright
paced back and forth like an expectant father. Sometimes he ran
on the spot or in small circles, beating his chest and waving his
arms, doing everything he could to keep warm. He did not dare
stop moving for fear of freezing to death.

The bundle secured to his liking, Helstone stood up and,
making sure his balance was good, threw the package to shore.
It arced across the water and landed in an explosion of snow,
clanking on rock. Wright quickly retrieved it, took out the
hatchet, and went into the forest for dry wood. Later, he came
back to the water's edge and called for more matches. This time

Will threw him a packet, shouting, "We don't have many left. If you can't get a fire started you'd better leave it until we can find a way to get to shore."

Try as he might, though, Wright could not get a fire going.

The day passed, and the men in the canoe could not think of a way to reach dry land. They had no rope left to throw to Wright and swimming was out of the question. Daylight had all but disappeared before the solution came to them, so simple that they chided themselves for not thinking of it sooner. They would *make* a rope. From the moosehide.

They ate a bit of beaver tail after throwing some to Wright, and prepared themselves for another miserable night in the canoe. Will felt great pity for Wright, whose situation was much more serious than theirs. Of all the people to be stranded on the shore alone, it had to be the one Will deemed the least capable of dealing with it. The young man had disappeared into the woods and, hearing the thwack, thwack of the hatchet above the sound of the river, they guessed what he was up to. He reappeared before darkness fell completely and told his companions that he had built a makeshift shelter and would see them in the morning. The woods swallowed him up again.

In the canoe, Will could not get Wright out of his mind. He did not know why, but he felt responsible for him in some way, and the heavy weight on his heart kept him awake for most of the night.

At first light Will and the others waved when Wright came out of the woods, limping and holding onto trees to keep his balance. "My toes are frozen," he shouted.

The only comfort they had to offer was to tell him of their strategy to get to shore. They threw him some more meat and half of their remaining matches. He devoured the food and failed again to light a fire.

Meanwhile, his companions took the moosehide that they had obtained from the Indians, which up until now had been used to protect their supplies from the rain and snow, and began cutting it into strips about an inch wide. They plaited these in lots of three, then tied them together, end to end. The men worked quickly, despite their cold fingers, and produced a rawhide rope that they hoped would be strong enough.

Next, they tied one end of a light cord to the rope and a stick fished from the river to the other end. Will threw the stick to shore, trailing the cord behind it, and instructed Wright to pull the rope to him and secure it around a tree. Wright, whose fingers felt as if they did not belong to him, found it impossible to pick up the stick and had to use his hands as pincers to accomplish the task. After a few fumbling attempts, he managed to form a half hitch around a small tree and, wrapping the rope around his wrists, pulled the knot tight.

Helstone volunteered to go first. He figured the rope was strong enough to get at least one person to shore but was not sure about the rest. He did not really care, though. They could swim and he could not. Will tied the rawhide around his waist with a bowline knot and then tied another long piece of light cord to the rope so that he could pull it back. "Wish me luck," Helstone said, taking the rope in his hands. He looked upriver to make sure there were no ice chunks or large pieces of driftwood to endanger him, then jumped into the icy water. He had a death grip on the rawhide, but even so, he nearly let go with the shock of the cold and the force of the current. It pushed him downstream, gasping and sputtering, until the rope stretched so taut that it looked as if it might snap, then pulled him under. He experienced a moment of panic and let go of the rope. Gagging on a mouthful of water, he fought his way to the surface, thrashing madly as he swung like a pendulum to shore. He hauled himself onto the bank, so cold he was scarcely able to breathe.

There was no time to waste. As quickly as his nearly useless fingers would allow, he worked at undoing the knot. He said later that a picture of the arthritic claws of some of the elderly hospital patients he had known flashed through his mind, and he knew the frustration they must have felt when they tried to use their fingers. He picked at the water-swollen knot for several moments, his teeth rattling from the cold, before he was finally able to loosen it. Wright was of no help to him.

Gilbert was next out of the canoe. Will retrieved the end of the rope by pulling on the cord, hand over hand. The frigid water made his fingers ache but he was immensely pleased at how well the rope strategy worked. As Gilbert did not know how to tie a bowline, Will did it for him, his fingers now as stiff as sticks. Once the rope was secure, Gilbert checked the river for debris and splashed in. Thomas went next; then, in two trips, Will sent over what was left of their food, clothing and blankets, along with a cooking pot, the two buffalo robes bought in Fort Edmonton and the remaining rifles and shotgun, using Thomas's deerskin each time to keep them dry. When he retrieved the rope for the final time, he did not know how he was able to tie the rawhide around his waist. He thought it was a bastardized version of a bowline knot that he had fashioned, but there seemed to be enough loops in it to hold. With a quick look upriver, he jumped in. The shock of the water forced his breath from him, and for a moment he thought he was drowning, that the river had him this time. But he came to the surface, the rope feeling strong, and moments later, he stood with his companions on the shore. He felt weak in the knees and did not know if it was from being cold or from the relief of feeling solid ground. Either way, they were still in desperate straits, and there was little room for debate on that point.

CHAPTER EIGHT

NOVEMBER 1862

Everyone except Wright, whose clothes were frozen, was sopping wet and shivering. There were not enough dry articles of clothing to provide a complete change for each man, but they divided what they had equally and prevented, temporarily at least, being turned into human icicles. No one had thought to bring mittens.

Wright could not change himself, so Helstone, who had helped many patients dress, gave him a hand. His nephew was clearly embarrassed by the process and said, "I feel like a child, Uncle."

"Tell me if you prefer feeling frozen, Johnny, and I'll stop," said Helstone.

Stung, Wright was silent.

Somehow, they had to get a fire going and make a decent shelter. Will and Thomas foraged in the dense spruce forest for firewood but could not find much that was ignitable. They collected what they could but wasted the last of their matches trying to get it to burn. They got only flameless smoke. They put making a fire aside for the time being and concentrated their efforts on building a shelter.

The place they had landed was a short but straight stretch of beach lined with rocks and deadfall of varying sizes. Behind the rocks was a thin, sparse line of tall cottonwood and shorter alder trees and, behind these, the brooding spruce forest. The men felt it was wise not to be too close to the river, in case it rose during the night, so at the inside edge of the forest, they cleared away the underbrush and arranged some deadfall in a crude "U" facing the river. Then they covered the top up with more deadfall, spruce boughs and the deerskin. It was not much, but it would at least protect them from everything but an east wind.

They huddled together in the shelter for warmth and pondered their situation. The good news was that they at least had a canoe, once they figured out a way to get it off the rock. The bad news was that it would not have much freeboard with the weight it would have to carry, and not enough rope to attach logs to improve it. The men discussed their options amid a general mood of despondency until Thomas observed that the level of the river had dropped perceptibly since yesterday. This caused a minor stir of excitement, and though it was too soon to celebrate, the sight of it boosted their spirits. If it went down far enough they might be able to build a bridge out to the canoe and dislodge it from its rocky perch. They would have to wait and see what the next day brought.

Despite the early hour, they kept to the shelter, wrapped in the blankets and buffalo robes. The warmth was minimal but better than none at all. Helstone wanted to know about the other canoe and asked Wright about his unexpected trip downriver.

He had held on to the overturned canoe, he told them, utterly terrified, and the icy water left him breathless. His heavy clothes threatened to drag him under and it had been a struggle just to keep his head above water and a grip on the vessel's slippery underside. He was afraid that if he let go he was doomed. Then he saw a rock looming ahead and, with no way of avoiding it, made a split-second decision: He pushed away from the canoe. He slid around one side of the boulder, missing it by inches, while the canoe smashed into it, side on. The angry waves carried the vessel around the far side of the rock, away from Wright, and it disappeared in the turbulent water. He had lost sight of it after that and did not know whether it had continued down the river or had sunk to the bottom. "Either way," he added, "everything on board was lost."

His immediate concern, though, was how to get to shore. He was too waterlogged to swim across the swift current, even if he knew how, so all he could do was let the river have its way with him, around one bend and then another. More than a mile downstream, he saw a point of small rocks jutting from the shore at a place where the river bent to his right and luckily, the current carried him straight toward it. On the far shore, he had noticed a high cutbank with trees perched precariously on its edge and had no idea why his mind registered that irrelevant information. He soon felt a slick, rocky bottom beneath his feet and stumbled to dry land, slipping on the rocks and bruising his knees and hands. He was so numb with cold he scarcely felt it. He was gasping for air so hard he thought he might choke, and it seemed to take forever to get his breath.

Exhausted and chilled to the very centre of his being, he said that he heard a rattling noise accompanied by an inhuman sound and thought he was about to be attacked by wild animals. Then he realized it was just himself moaning through madly clacking teeth. He stood up, flapped his arms and danced up and down, trying to restore some warmth to his body. When he felt that his blood was circulating again, he had carefully begun working his way along the treacherous shore, full of slippery, snow-covered rocks and deadfall, back upriver, fearful that he would find his companions' numbers reduced by two. As far as he knew, Helstone and Will had gone into the river with him. He had felt panicky and utterly alone and had to keep himself from rushing. The last thing he needed was a twisted or broken ankle. When he saw four people waving at him from the canoe, he felt weak-kneed with relief. "I thought we might have lost you, Uncle," he said, but Helstone gave only a noncommittal grunt.

Trying to get a fire going had been the most frustrating experience in his life. He could not find any decent firewood, so he had chipped bark from a tree and hoped that would work. "But my hands were so numb, I couldn't feel the matches. I kept breaking the damned things at first, and then when I finally got one going, the bark chips wouldn't light." When the last match was gone, he had kicked the pile of chips in anger and frustration. He swore at his clumsy hands and at himself for being so blockheaded as to come on this journey in the first place.

He had felt near to collapsing, he was so weary. He hacked branches from the trees and with part of them formed a bed beneath the shelter of some deadfall. The rest he had used as covers. It was scarcely adequate, but he had been too tired to care. He passed out moments after he pulled the last branch on top of him.

"It didn't last long, though," Wright said. "Last night was the most miserable night of my life."

He had awakened cold, with a feeling of pins and needles in his feet, but he did not have the energy to get up and move around. He tried wiggling his toes, but it was too hard and he eventually gave up. He stuffed his fingers into his armpits and spent the remainder of the interminable night slipping in and out of another world. Mostly, he thought of Elizabeth and their two lovely daughters, both so young he feared that they would not even remember him when he came home. If he made it home. Several times during the night, he thought he might never see them again. Such depressing thoughts had invariably returned him to his world of ice, snow and spruce boughs. He looked at Helstone and with some bitterness said, "What a bloody fool I was, Uncle, to ever let you talk me into coming."

If Helstone felt any compassion for his nephew, it did not show. "We all make our own choices, Johnny," he said. "You can't blame a little bit of bad luck on me."

Wright turned his sad eyes toward Gilbert and Thomas. "You don't know how many times I've wished I was back at the shoe factory," he said. "Do you remember how hot it could get during the summer? That's what I wanted most of all. Besides Elizabeth and the children."

He had awakened dreaming of them, and when he placed his hands on the ground to push himself up, he had no feeling in his toes. They had frozen during the night.

It was on this disconsolate note that the conversation ended. Wright's voice had been trembling as he spoke, and it seemed to Will that he was on the verge of breaking down completely. It's a good thing, he thought, that we've almost reached our destination.

The men drifted off into their own thoughts. They passed another wretched night that held only two small mercies for Will: He was not in the canoe, and the sound of the river was off to the side instead of all around him.

Come morning, patches of ice-fog hung above the river interspersed with blue sky. Will did not know the exact temperature, but it was definitely below zero. Thomas moaned;

he could not feel his toes, and Helstone, who had just awakened, voiced the same complaint. Will could only think of his younger brother's remonstrations about their late departure from London. He gripped the young man's shoulder.

"Not to worry, Tommy," he said. He had not called his brother that since they were children, but it had slipped out because he suddenly felt so protective of him. "We'll get a fire going. I'd bet my Henry on it."

He hoped his words sounded more positive to Thomas's ears than they did to his own, but he had an idea and could have kicked himself for not thinking of it sooner. It was yet another indication that all of them were totally out of their element. They had no business being here on this river in this strange land. They were shoemakers and a hospital worker, not woodsmen, and this simple fact might yet be the death of them.

Will instructed Gilbert to gather the smallest twigs he could find along with some slightly larger pieces of wood. Then he cut a one-inch strip from the edge of his blanket. He repeated the process with the rest of the blankets, then cut the strips into 12-inch lengths and, as they had done with the rawhide, plaited them in lots of three. Once that was done, they had dry kindling. Next, he dug a flint and striker out of his pack, along with a couple of bullets. He took these and, with the kindling, went outside to where Gilbert had made a circular fire pit with rocks. Beside the pit was a neat pile of the twigs and wood he had gathered. Will took out a dry handkerchief, crumpled it up and placed it in the pit. With his knife, he pried the casings from the bullet heads and dumped the gunpowder into a depression in the handkerchief. Then he frayed the end of one of the pieces of kindling. He said to his brother, "You hold the frayed end of the kindling over the powder while I try to ignite it." It took several strikes of the flint before the gunpowder ignited and the handkerchief and kindling caught on fire, but when they did, they burned well. Other pieces were added to the tiny blaze, the smaller twigs and successively bigger pieces until there was a sustainable blaze going. Even Gilbert, who was not given to emotional displays, cheered and the others came out of the shelter to surround the miracle of fire. It began to snow again, the flakes dropping straight down out of a grey sky, but the flames leapt high and the warmth they sent out felt like summer in the Canadas.

They made tea and again discussed their circumstances, which the tea and the warmth of the fire had greatly improved. Their food supply, most of which had gone downriver, was critically low and would definitely need supplementing with the occasional small animal. That they had seen none was worrisome, but then they had not really been looking. The river was continually dropping, and if it carried on at the same pace, it might be soon be possible to build a bridge out to the canoe to salvage it. That, of course, would be the best of all possible worlds as Helstone, Wright and Thomas all had frostbite; they could walk, but the lack of feeling in their feet affected their balance. The river, then, was their only pathway to the safety of Fort George. They would wait until tomorrow and hope that it would co-operate.

While they talked, the frostbitten men removed their boots and tried to restore circulation by massaging their feet, which made them itch and burn fiercely. Wright's toes were the worst and looked pale and waxy; the others' were not quite as severely frozen. Wright took some salve out of the small satchel of medical supplies he had brought with him and slathered some on his feet while Will and Gilbert heaped a supply of wood beside the fire. Between the two of them, they would have to keep it going throughout the night.

Nobody got much sleep. The men tossed and turned and the little slumber they got was anxiety-ridden and restless. The shelter was hard and cramped, but it at least forced the men close together and gave them warmth — a relative term, to be sure, but better than full exposure to the cold or being alone under the buffalo robes. Even so, the night was misery intensified by fear of the unknown.

Beyond the moans and sniffs of his companions, Will listened to the river wend its mindless path south. It seemed to him that it was no longer flowing with same force. God knows he had heard it enough over the past two and a half weeks and was familiar with its sound — far more than he had ever wanted to be, and that was a fact. At first light, he crawled from beneath the buffalo robe and walked to the river's edge, trying to work the stiffness out of his body and some warmth into it. What he saw was both reassuring and distressing: a large, flat rock now jutted up from the water, a little more than half the distance to the canoe, which was now nearly high and dry. This meant that they could build a bridge out to it, but it also meant that the river was down because it was freezing. As proof, there were patches of ice in the quieter places along the shore. Excited, he returned to the others to share the good news. Despair fell from them like rain off a slicker. The three with frostbite forgot their woes for the time being and exulted in the positive turn of events. At last, there was a good chance that they would escape this Godforsaken place.

"Come on, Gilbert," Will said. "We've got work to do."

Since the two brothers were the only ones completely mobile, the job of building a bridge fell to them. Will grabbed the hatchet — their big axe had been lost when the first canoe capsized — and they quickly selected four trees about 8 to 10 inches in diameter and felled them. It was a laborious task with the small tool, but they took turns, working slowly so that they did not sweat too much. Their breath came out in visible puffs in the chill air as they worked, and by late morning the trees were on the ground, trimmed, and cut to a length that would reach the first rock — about 25 feet. One at a time, they dragged them to the river, stood them up and let them fall onto the exposed rock. Once they had all four logs side by side, which took a little maneuvering, Gilbert crawled out to the centre of the span and tied them together with a short length cut from the moosehide rope. The structure was unsteady but it worked.

Even though the gap between the first and second rock was shorter, the task of spanning it was more challenging, as the brothers had to negotiate the shaky bridge carrying heavy logs. Nonetheless, they soon had the second span secured and were standing beside the canoe.

They had secured one end of the moosehide rope to a tree on shore, and now tied the other end to the canoe. Once that was done, they began trying to dislodge it from its perch. The footing was treacherous, but the slippery rock also worked in their favour, and the canoe splashed into the water and swung to shore on its tether, just as the men had done two days previously. Those on shore shouted in jubilation.

It was a victory of immeasurable magnitude. The only thing that could have made it better was if they had been able to leave right away. But it had taken too long to fell the trees and build the bridges, and it was much too late in the day to think about packing the canoe and setting off. It would have to wait until morning, but their morale was up and they had fire, so they could handle one more night in this dreadful place. Then they would quit it forever.

It began snowing again around suppertime and a north wind grew boisterous, piling the snow up in small drifts. Regardless, there was much optimism in the shelter that night as the men huddled together. They talked of gold, but mostly they talked of their families, who, they knew, would be worried. Yet there was some comfort in the thought that their loved ones were mercifully unaware of their predicament. Chewing on moose jerky as tough as old leather, they reflected on past meals but also spoke confidently of the future. They were obviously going to arrive in Cariboo much too late for the mining season, but were reasonably assured of getting there. Considering the events of the past few days, that would be no small feat.

Snow fell all night and the river grew even quieter. In the morning, ice covered more of its surface and the drifts on the exposed shore were calf-deep. The men knew that they would have to work quickly. Wright complained of frostbite in his fingers and his palms were turning numb. It was almost a whimper, but he caught himself before it became embarrassing.

Will and Gilbert packed the canoe carefully. Not only would it have to carry what was left of their drastically reduced supplies, it would have to carry five men as well. Once they had the packing done to their mutual satisfaction, they helped Wright to the vessel and placed him amidships, making him as comfortable as possible in the limited space available. Then they assisted the rest of their companions aboard. The last thing they did, before climbing in themselves, was pile extra wood on the fire just in case the river had iced up and forced them to turn back. Then Gilbert took the bow, Will the stern, and they pushed off with the paddles, careful not to rock the vessel too much. The small amount of freeboard would not tolerate it.

The river did not look good at all. It had slowed considerably, and ice swirled around them in large and small chunks that banged into the canoe. Despite the nerve-wracking sound and the trembling of the canoe, the slow river was a boon with the vessel riding so low in the water. They had just rounded the first bend when they came upon an ice jam forming a wall across the river.

There had been no further talk about cannibalism. Most of the days were spent in complete silence, since all of the important things had already been said. Despite the inclement weather, they had managed to keep the fire going, though sometimes it seemed to be more smoke than fire. They almost lost it entirely a couple of times when he had fallen asleep during his watch. His companions ranted at him and had they each been stronger, the arguments might have come to blows. They were still able to gather wood, although each gathering required going farther and farther afield, a monumental task for all of them. With each passing day their appearance grew more haggard; he himself sometimes felt like a doddering old man. Nevertheless, they persevered. Nearly as much as the sparse rations they had had, it was the fire's warmth and the light it shed in the black nights that kept them going. It was the heart of their existence, reminding them of better times, and they knew it was probably worth their lives to let it go out.

They had decided some time ago to sleep together for warmth, often embracing each other as if they were lovers and taking turns at the centre position once each night. Such intimacy among men felt awkward at first, but the practicality of it soon overcame their inhibitions. Before long, the centre spot became the most coveted, for it was only then that the men felt even remotely warm, front and back. They made sure that they emptied their bladders before settling in for the night, to reduce the need for movement even further. But the nights were long, and it could be safely predicted that he, at least, would at some point disturb everyone to go relieve himself. It never failed to annoy the others.

One night, after a bitter wind and the driving snow had stopped, when the stars glittered like shards of crystal in the heavens and ice had reduced the sound of the rapids to a gurgle, they heard wolves howling in the distance. The haunting sound gripped them with fear. What could they do if they were attacked by a pack of the beasts and their weapons failed in the cold weather? Their next line of defense was their knives, sturdy and lethal bowies, which might be all right to fight off one animal, but what about several of them? He did not think he was up to it; he was too weak and so were his companions. Despite their weapons, they felt handicapped and defenseless, easy prey for any predatory animal.

There was no way around the ice and no place to cut through it. It was as impenetrable as steel. They paddled to shore and Gilbert waded through the snow to investigate conditions on the far side of the jam. His heart fell into his gut. All he could see was more ice. He returned to the canoe with the discouraging news that a river passage to Fort George was no longer an option. There was a stony silence in the canoe as they pushed away from the shore and paddled back the way they had come, their crushing disappointment obvious in the droop of their shoulders.

The sluggish river allowed them to make the return trip without difficulty, and the campfire smoked and crackled merrily, as if mocking the men for their failure to escape this desolation.

"Gilbert and I will have to go for help," Will said, once they had all gathered around the fire. "We sure as hell can't sit around here waiting for spring, and we're the only ones healthy enough to do it."

"Do you think it's necessary?" asked Thomas. "Sooner or later some Indians are bound to pass through here on their way to the fort. They'll probably have some food to leave us and they'll be able to send help once they get there." He was anxious about splitting the party up and hated the thought of being separated from his brothers.

"You are a trusting soul," said Helstone, without trying to hide his sarcasm. "They'd more likely steal the few belongings we have left. Maybe even kill us, if they didn't leave us to die."

"It can't be more than 35 or 40 miles to Fort George," Will broke in, trying to prevent the discussion from dissolving into an argument. "If Gilbert and I leave first thing tomorrow morning, we should be able to get there in five days. That's covering only seven or eight miles a day. We might even get there sooner if we make better time. At the outside, we ought to be back with help in 10 days. If you boys ration yourselves, there's enough food to last that long, maybe even longer if you're lucky enough to bag an animal. All Gilbert and I will take with us is a ration of fat each."

They talked about whether Will should take the Henry or leave it behind in camp for the others to use. The consensus was that it should go with him and that Gilbert should take Helstone's shotgun. Other than the fat, the brothers would be without food and therefore would need the most effective weapons to obtain it. If they were not able to kill some kind of bird or animal along the way, it was going to be a long, hungry haul to Fort George.

Their differences notwithstanding, they had been constant companions for nearly six months, through good times and bad, so the decision to break up was an emotionally wrenching one. It was a collision between the heart and the mind, and the mind won as it had to. Will and Gilbert would leave the following morning to bring back help.

So that those staying behind might avoid the arduous task, Will and Gilbert spent the remainder of the day cutting and collecting firewood, mostly driftwood and deadfall from up and down the shore. They stacked it up next to the fire for easy access, and by the time darkness fell, they were exhausted. They hoped they had accumulated enough to last until their return.

In the morning, the sky was a grey down quilt, torn apart, dumping its white, feathery contents onto the ground, and there was even more ice on the river. Visibility was only a few hundred yards. The men silently ate a meagre breakfast, and the brothers gathered up their rations of fat, the moosehide rope, two machetes, a hatchet, the Henry, the shotgun and the blankets, leaving the buffalo robes in camp. Thomas wanted to read a brief passage from his Bible, and since the moment seemed appropriate, the others agreed.

"In the beginning," he read, "was the Word and the Word was with God, and the Word was God. All things were made by Him, and without Him was not anything made that was made. In Him was life, and the life was the light of men. And the light shineth in the darkness. Amen."

And will continue to shine, thought Will hopefully, especially in this particular darkness. He felt awkward saying goodbye. It was hard to leave these men behind, even Helstone, who should have been easy. Thomas looked downcast and it pulled at Will's heart.

"We'll be back as quick as we can," he said, and nearly choked on the words. It was an awesome responsibility that he and Gilbert were charged with and he prayed they were up to the task. The lives of the men they were leaving behind depended on it. The life of his brother depended on it. He sought Thomas's eyes with his own and held them for a moment, saying there the words that his tongue could not speak.

He looked from Thomas to the others. They were in horrible condition, like beggars in want of a good home and a decent meal. He wondered if they had 10 days' survival left in them.

"If you have any sense at all," said Wright, "you'll send someone else back and stay away from this place. No one here would blame you if that's what you did. That's what I would do." Of the three men staying behind, he was in the worst shape.

Of course, that's what *you'd* do, thought Will. But it isn't what I would do. "We'd better go," he said, restless with urgency and wanting to quit this desperate scene as quickly as possible. The two brothers turned and put the camp and their companions at their backs.

"Lord have mercy on us all," cried Helstone.

The others called "Godspeed" as the brothers waved and disappeared like ghostly shadows into the falling snow.

Part Three

THE SEPARATION

CHAPTER NINE

NOVEMBER 1862

Winter was setting in hard and fast as Will and Gilbert picked their way along the river. At first, the beach was relatively flat and would have been easy to follow without any snow, but the snow presented two problems: It was not frozen hard enough to support them, but it was deep enough to hide rocks and deadfall. Thus, they moved slowly, not needing an injury to add to their problems.

The brothers did not get far on the first day of their journey. Indeed, Will guessed that they might have covered only three or four miles at best, and he thought he was being generous with that estimate. They debated whether they should use up some of their ammunition to light a fire and voted in favour of it. Even though their blankets were warm, their clothes were wet and needed drying out. They were ravenous, too, but knew that their bodies would need the fat and its benefits more at some point in the future than now, so they went without food. They hoped that sitting still for a while might fool some animal into believing the area was safe, but nothing came of it. Huddled together for extra warmth, they talked — they could not help themselves — of home and of those back at the campsite.

"I can't tell you how many times I wished we could have left Helstone behind," said Gilbert, "but I never dreamed of anything like this. Yet I sometimes wonder if I'd be anywhere near as desperate to get help back to them if Thomas wasn't there."

Will wondered, too, but said only, "What does it matter? And if we can't put more miles behind us than we did to today, there's not much hope for any of them." It was a bleak thought on which to spend the night.

There was no wind, and the snow dropped like stones from the sky all through the first day and continued through the night as well. Come morning, it showed no signs of letting up. By noon, the brothers were wading crotch-deep in it, and they had to spell each other off from the onerous task of breaking a trail. Rest stops became more frequent. This slowed them even further and made their pace the day before seem fast by comparison. Then a steep rocky point brought them to an abrupt halt. They could not traverse it for fear of falling into the river. The land on their right rose a good hundred feet above them, precipitous and not climbable in this weather, so they retraced their steps to a place where the slope was less steep and there were plenty of trees to assist them in their passage. Along the way, a small avalanche of snow slid down and buried them up to their waists. They stoically dug themselves out and continued on, having already accepted the tyranny of the land as an unpleasant force in their lives.

It was a tough climb up the slope to the top, and once there they stayed well away from the edge, for it looked dangerously unstable in spots. They entered the sepulchral silence of the forest where there was not as much snow, but it was gloomy and ominous. The underbrush was thick in places, and they cleared a path with the machete, always taking turns to share the workload. They were careful not to penetrate the forest too deeply for fear of losing their bearings. The last thing they wanted was to have to retrace their steps.

They came upon a ravine, obviously once a creek, that was perhaps 30 or 40 feet deep, its bottom lined with snow-laden scrub alder. It sloped toward the river, which was where they preferred to be.

"I'm all for getting back to the river where we can see where were going," said Gilbert.

"You won't get any argument from me," said Will. He hated being in the forest with its half-light and limited visibility.

But it was too dangerous to descend into the ravine from where they stood, so they followed it deeper into the forest. They had gone more than a quarter of a mile before they found a suitable place.

Making their way down the ravine was torturous. They slipped and floundered through the twining alder whose only reason for existing seemed to be to thwart their forward progress. Branches whipped at their faces and snow fell on them in huge lumps from above. Sometimes they had to beat their way down, hacking away with the machete as if possessed by demons, unwilling to stop for a rest until they were back beside the river. Will tried not to think that their hard work would go unrewarded, that the river shore would be impassable once they got there. When they stumbled from the ravine and saw the river, grey and uninviting, it was like encountering a familiar face in a strange city, and it gladdened them no small degree.

Luckily, the beach proved to be relatively flat and wide and, after a short rest, they made good time for a while. Then the river began to curve sharply to their left, and in that curve was a massive cutbank that ran for perhaps a quarter of a mile and rose a hundred feet or more in treeless, snowy folds. The shoreline narrowed to a thread in front of it so that there was not much room between its slope and the water. The footing became treacherous.

"Maybe we should go back a ways and see if there's a spot where we can climb back up the bluff," Gilbert suggested.

"I don't recall seeing one," said Will. "If there isn't then we'll have to go back to the ravine and that doesn't appeal to me one bit. I don't know about you, but I've seen the only ravine that I want to see for today."

"But what if we can't get past at the other end?"

"We'll worry about that when we get there," Will said. "Right now we're wasting time."

Painstakingly, they worked their way along the base of the cutbank, folded in some places like the bellows of an accordion. Beneath the inner parts of the fold, there was an ample amount of beach, but on the outer portions, the men were mere inches from the river, and had to lean into the bank for support. Occasionally, small avalanches of snow fell around them but were not troublesome. Their biggest worry was of slipping into the murky water. They had no idea how deep it was, but even shallow water would soak their feet through and that would be catastrophic.

As they neared the last of the folds, Will could see that the trail ahead did not look very promising. The cutbank ended at a little cove where the beach was much wider, but beyond that was a shoulder of rock undercut by the river, which swirled menacingly around its base and blocked their way. Without a word, they turned and began retracing the long route back to the ravine. Will appreciated that Gilbert, even though he may have been thinking it, refrained from saying, "I told you so."

On the south side of the ravine, the forest was not as dense and there were many wide-open spaces amongst the trees. And since the brothers were as spent as the daylight, they camped in the shelter of a half-dozen spruce clumped together as if they needed protection from the elements, as if they too found strength in numbers.

They pushed on at first light, the river far below them on one side and a monotony of spruce on the other. It was always hard to get moving, as they were stiff and sore from sleeping on the ground, but a couple of hundred yards over the rugged terrain was usually enough to clear out the kinks until the next morning. Despite the physical demands on their bodies, which cried out for more nourishment, the brothers held off eating their single ration of fat, feeding instead on rosehips when the seed pods were available. They also held off lighting fires in order to save their ammunition for game. If they got lucky and shot something, they would light a fire to cook it, but only then.

The weather began to change; a stiff breeze blew the clouds away and the sky was a brilliant blue. It raised their spirits, and there were places where they could get out of the biting breeze and actually feel the sun's scant warmth. It was still bitterly cold at night.

The next day they came upon the tracks of a small animal and followed them. Neither of the brothers had enough experience to know what kind of animal had made them but it mattered little in the end. The tracks disappeared into an impenetrable jungle of undergrowth and could not be picked up again. Even so, they found some comfort in those tracks, because they indicated the presence of other life forms in this God-forgotten part of the world.

Gradually, the terrain became more open and allowed for good visibility. The downside was deep snow that made them feel as if they were walking with lead weights in their shoes. The ground, though, was obviously sloping gently toward the level of the river, for they were not as high above it as they once were. By late afternoon, they were only a few feet from the water and had entered a broad, relatively flat clearing, with patches of scrub trees amongst acres of bush. Ahead, the top half of a long line of barren trees stretched off to the northwest, and it took a moment for the meaning of it to register in Will's consciousness.

"I think those trees ahead mark a river," he said. He could not keep the excitement from his voice.

"Then it must be the Nechako!" Gilbert was more than willing to believe such a claim despite the absence of proof.

The brothers hurried forward, their pace quickened by the possibility of what lay ahead. They reached the line of trees and broke through, and there before them was an unfordable river flowing into the Fraser. On the far side were more trees and hills.

"Where in Hell is the fort?" Gilbert grumbled, disappointed that it was not plainly visible. "It's marked on the map as being right at the confluence."

"It's probably downstream, hidden by the trees. It'd be flooded out every spring if they'd built it over there."

A part of Will wanted to believe what he had just said, but another part, the one that did not like to invest too much in emotions, harboured doubts. But then again, the Nechako *was* the only tributary shown on their map. Surely, a river of this size would have been marked. Not only that, the scale on the map was poor enough that the fort could easily be a half-mile or more downstream.

"That must be it," Gilbert said. "They probably found a better building site down a bit."

"Let's hope so. Whatever the case, we can't cross here."

The river's mouth swirled with deep water and was near 75 feet in breadth. They would have to follow its course, which bent to the northwest, to find a safe ford.

One of the small comforts they had enjoyed at the beginning of their ordeal was their tobacco. They had made it last a long time by rationing it as strictly as they had their food, but it was all gone now. For a while, they had clamped their teeth around their tobaccoless pipes or held them in their hands for the familiarity, but gradually, as their bodies were weaned from the nicotine, that crutch was no longer necessary.

He still had plenty of worries though; there was no shortage in that department. Mostly he worried about death. He was afraid of it, even more of the means of dying. He feared an attack by wolves, his body torn to shreds with his mind fully aware of what was happening. He feared, too, an attack by Indians, and sometimes he feared going to sleep, feared the nightmares or simply not waking up ever again. And he feared the demonic voices that echoed in his head when he fell into a daytime stupor. It was only his faith in God that rescued him, and he would come alive shouting words in His name.

He was astonished at how emaciated his body looked; he did not need a mirror, he could see it in his arms and legs, how his raggedy clothes hung on him. Yet there burned in him like a gas lamp, an incredible will to live. The key to survival, he knew, was having faith that he would survive.

They stayed between the line of trees and the riverbank, wading on through the deep snow that softened the look of the land but made it harder to traverse without snowshoes. By nightfall, the river was still too wide for crossing, so they went into the forest where the snow was not as deep, made a shelter and waited out another long night.

At dawn, they ate their ration of fat. Not only did their bodies need it, but they had both concluded that this was indeed the Nechako and that Fort George was only a short distance down the Fraser from the confluence. They believed that as soon as they could find a ford, they would be on the last leg of their journey. Best of all, they could send help back to Thomas and the others, who by now would be halfway through their rations.

In some places, the banks sloped steeply down to the river, and they had to hang on to tree branches to keep from slipping into the water. In other places, where the river bent away from them, they would find a small beach strewn with rocks and littered with driftwood, all slippery with snow and ice. One place wanted to send you into the river to for a good soaking or to drown, the other wanted to break your ankles. Will did not know which he hated worse. Hated this bloody country, actually, for it was doing its damndest to thwart them both.

On their second day on the tributary it finally seemed to be narrowing, but was still too deep and swift to cross. There were plenty of rosehips, though, and they feasted on them during their breaks and gathered up as many as they could carry for less plentiful times. The hips were not very tasty, but it was amazing how an empty, growling stomach could turn them into something palatable.

They fought their way upstream, for it was indeed a battle now, the brothers against the terrain, the weather which had soured again, and their gnawing hunger. Late in the day, they found what they were looking for.

They had reached a place where the river was split into three narrow channels by two small islands. Using a series of rocks as stepping stones, they reached the first island, and on the far side, the wider, unfordable middle channel was spanned by a fallen cottonwood, slick with ice and unstable at its narrow end, but useable nonetheless. On the other side of the second island was the main channel of the river, wide and deep, with no possible way to ford it, and no trees tall enough on the island to span it. It looked as if they would have either to go back to the north bank and search further upstream for a suitable crossing place or figure out how to build a bridge.

It did not take them long to decide. They discovered that some of the trees along the shore of the island were almost tall enough to bridge the gap to the mainland, so the next morning they selected the tallest one closest to the river's edge and cut it just enough to topple it. It splashed into the water and floated there, anchored to its stump by its strong outer rings, the top end not more than 9 or 10 feet from the far shore. Next, they cut down four shorter trees, which they stripped of their branches and carried to the fallen tree. One at a time, the logs were put in the water, maneuvered out to the end, and pushed toward the far shore until they lodged in the sediment a foot or so from dry land. They were then lifted by rope onto the tree and tied there. Finished, the structure was wobbly but stable enough to get them to the mainland. They had used up three precious days, though, trying to cross the uncharted river.

They did not get far downriver that afternoon before running out of daylight. One particularly rough section of the shoreline required more machete work than their energy reserves allowed. Nevertheless, they camped that night with a modicum of optimism that if the trail improved they might be able to reach the fort the following afternoon. Or the next at the very latest.

Next morning, Will awoke first, his brain foggy until he heard what he thought was a twig snapping. He was instantly alert; it might be an animal. He carefully picked up his rifle. Gilbert was just waking up, so Will motioned him to be quiet. With all the stealth he could muster from his cold body, he worked himself into a position where he could see beyond the rim of their shelter. Not more than three yards distant was a skunk, the black part of its fur stark against the snow. He could not remember when a target had seemed so small. It had just raised itself up on its haunches to sniff the air when Will shot it. He had aimed for its body, but the bullet tore through the animal's neck, nearly severing its head. This turned out to be another stroke of good luck, for the lead had spoiled none of the meat.

They were able to gather a few dry twigs in their little hollow and lit a fire with gunpowder and their last handkerchief. The skunk stank to high heaven and tasted almost as bad, but it was food and would sustain them for another day and more. Late that afternoon, Gilbert brought down two grouse with the shotgun and the brothers had another feast, eating one bird and saving the other for breakfast.

They had recognized a big boulder across the river, which indicated that there was still some distance to go to the confluence. The following morning, with their energy level the best it had been for some time, they reached the Fraser in short order and in good spirits. They turned south once more, expecting to reach the fort at any moment. But the morning passed, as did the afternoon, and the fort did not appear. Nor did it the next day and the next. They saw nothing, save the immutable wilderness.

CHAPTER TEN

NOVEMBER 1862

The tributary that they had followed for so many days was uncharted, and Will wished a plague on all mapmakers for their incompetence. How could they have missed such a broad river? Yet they had, and when the reality of this awful fact sank into their dulling minds, it was depressing beyond imagining. It began to look like the Indians had been telling the truth when they said it was a five-day paddle from their encampment to the fort, and not two days as Will had thought. He supposed that they should know such things, but he really thought they had been lying to strengthen their bargaining position. He tried to add up the days since they left their companions and could not remember all of them. Whatever the figure was, he knew one thing with absolute certainty: unless they had shot something, Thomas and the others would be out of food by now.

He and Gilbert were starving again, too. They had not seen any more animals, and they had run out of rosehips. Though the seed pods were never filling, they at least prevented scurvy, an advantage now lost to them.

They climbed a flat-topped knoll above the river to see if they could catch even the smallest indication of humankind: an Indian encampment, perhaps, or maybe smoke rising from a trapper's cabin. Even the fort itself would not be too much to ask for. But all they saw were forested, snow-covered hills stretching away in all directions, bisected by the endless river.

The weather was the only thing working in their favour lately. It had even grown milder, which had helped, but now low black clouds scudded across the sky and the temperature plummeted. The wind grew mean and bullied the treetops, and was so cold it all but sucked the breath right out of the brothers.

It began to snow again, first lightly, in stony pellets whipped around by the wind, and then furiously, a blinding blizzard that drove them into the forest to seek shelter. For two days the storm raged and imprisoned them, for they did not have the strength to hack their way through the undergrowth.

On the third day, they were able to get underway again. The wind had ceased and the snow fell gently, adding to the massive drifts formed during the storm. On average, the snow was waist-deep, but some drifts were over the brothers' heads and they had to dig their way through when they could not pass in the forest.

Gilbert looked miserable, but his quiet nature rarely let him complain, which was all right with Will. He had his own misery to contend with. Will presumed that he, himself, probably did not look much better than his brother did. Maybe even worse, particularly if he looked anything like he felt. The pair of them stank, too, a fact never more evident than when they were under their blankets. When a man can smell himself, Will thought, he has to be in a bad way.

Slowly, the famished pair moved along the river's edge, following its twists and turns, embittered every time that they knew the river was doubling back on itself and had therefore added several more punishing miles to their journey.

On one occasion, they observed tracks of a small animal, on another a bird, but saw nothing of the creatures themselves. Once, a raven or large crow winged its solitary way overhead, within shooting range, but had Gilbert been lucky enough to bring it down with the shotgun, it would have landed in the river. It disappeared over the trees on the far bank. Then in quick order, Gilbert shot a grouse and Will a mink, small victories in what was beginning to look like a losing battle. They skinned both creatures and were so ravenous that they ate them raw and drank the warm blood. It was satisfying at first, to have something of substance going into their bellies, but before long, cramps came. The meat so disagreed with them that it turned their bowels into water. Several times, they had to stop to relieve themselves right where they stood and were fortunate to get their trousers down. Gilbert complained that his guts felt as if he someone had stabbed them with a ragged-edge knife. Will offered no sympathy; his felt the same.

On a part of the river that was running almost due west, they came to what they thought was another tributary, deep and uncrossable. For a moment, they believed it might be the Nechako, but since the slight current was running inland, they realized it must be a back channel instead. The water was quiet enough that they might have been able to cross it with some semblance of a raft had they not used up their rope crossing the tributary. With no other option, they followed the shore. When at last they had worked their way back to the main channel of the river, they could see the spot where they had once stood, not more than 20 yards away. But four more tortured days had passed.

Time became meaningless. In the beginning they had kept their watches wound but had let them lapse somewhere along the way. Their progress was no longer measured in time anyway. It was measured in distance, by placing one foot in front of the other until they had gone a yard, a rod, a quarter-mile, a half-mile, a mile. Of course, they had no means of determining if they had gone one mile or 10, only that they had made progress because they had spent the day placing one foot in front of the other. Neither of the brothers had any notion of how many days had passed since they left the rapids. For Will, time had frozen into blocks of gruelling days and long cruel nights, separated only by memorable incidents like the tributary, the back channel and those days they were able to obtain food. For the life of him, he could not recollect how many days and nights each block contained, only that too many of them had passed, which no doubt spelled trouble for those they had left behind. And sometimes he cared little about that.

His head ached from lack of food and a great knot in his stomach made him feel like vomiting. His mouth was dry, as if it were stuffed with wool. He was lethargic and only kept moving forward, once he got started, because it seemed easier than stopping and getting started all over again. His legs were weak and quivery and his movements felt as tentative as a newborn colt's. His fingers seemed as thick as sausages.

Sausages. Just like the ones his mother brought home from Beales' butcher shop, fat and aromatic, sizzling in the frying pan. He could almost smell them.

Small thoughts like that gave him moments of delirium, his mind seeking refuge in hallucinations of home. Once, while climbing over a large snow-covered stump, he fell off the other side. He moaned as he rose from the snow and did not know where he was. A face came into his blurred vision that he instantly recognized. It was his mother, smiling above him against the backdrop of a brilliant sun, the corona encircling her head like the Madonna and her halo.

"Jesus Christ, Mother," he asked. "Where the Hell am I?"

He immediately regretted his strong language and wanted to apologize, but the words would not form, so lost was he in her beauty. That she had managed to find her way to this savage place filled him with awe but not surprise, and the love he had felt for her before paled by comparison with what filled him now. How much did he owe her? He owed her everything. If there was any good in him, it had flowed through her. If he owned any single trait that might allow him to pass muster on Judgment Day, if there was such a thing, it had come from her. Now her face was becoming blurry, and when his eyes returned to focus, it was only his brother's face that he saw: bearded, blue eyes red-rimmed and saturated with distress.

Gilbert was shaking him, "You're with me, Will. You're with me. We're here together, and I need you. We need each other, Will."

He wanted to weep for his loss.

When he fell down for the third or fourth time in less than an hour, he seriously considered not rising again. His legs wanted to give out, and he was weary beyond all comprehension. Wherever the fort was, it was too far and to reach it would require strength he no longer possessed. What had he come here for? Gold? Adventure? New challenges? Surely not this kind of challenge, a game in which if you lose you die. Dying. Dead. Death. The thought of it crept into his mind more often than he liked. He had felt Death dogging his every step for some time now, so why not just embrace him and be done with it? The snow almost felt warm, and he reckoned that it would provide as good a tomb as any that a man with great wealth could afford. All he had to do was lie down and stay there, and in time he would disappear from this earth, go some place where he would no longer have to face the pitiless wind and the hard pellets of snow that blasted his face like sand.

Yet even though a part of his mind accepted the stark fact of death, another part would not allow it. Some primeval urge bade him rise up and keep moving, which he did by taking one step at a time through the merciless snow and the penetrating cold.

How could a body be so cold, he wondered, and still function, still survive? He did not know. He knew only that there was not a single place within him that did not recognize the cold as victor, did not bow down to its supremacy. Movement, then, was the difference between life and death, but the cold was always there, snapping at his heels like some savage animal determined to devour him. So move he did, around each bend, and another, where there was always more snow and the never-ending cold. If there's country worse than this, Will thought, it's not likely I'll ever live to see it.

Winter days were short at this latitude and the long nights were a vast dark plain with an invisible horizon. The sun, when it shone, never showed itself until 8:30 in the morning and was gone before four o'clock in the afternoon. On dismal days, when the clouds draped the hilltops, which was the case more often than not, the daylight never seemed to brighten much beyond early twilight.

Having to spend many of their waking hours in darkness was depressing, and their only solace was the flickering light of the fire and its radiant warmth. To some degree, the fire sustained them, like the few drops of dew that kept a man from dying of thirst in the desert. Their control over it was a link to their humanity, the fire itself, perhaps, a link to God. Without it, they were scarcely different from the rest of the animals that roamed this wilderness. Without it, their ability to survive would be seriously breached.

The brothers rarely spoke anymore, so preoccupied were they with survival. Yet it did not matter to either of them; each other's presence was what they really needed. When Gilbert collapsed in the snow, panic squeezed Will's heart and did not let up until several minutes after his brother had revived.

When they made camp, often no more than wrapping themselves in their blankets in whatever shelter they could find, the oppressive silence of the land almost crushed them. It was enough to drive a man stark raving mad. Will would have screamed to fill the void with something human, but he did not have a scream left in him.

In the darkness, the emotions that often deserted him during the day would come to the fore and tears would fill the corners of his eyes. It was funny, he thought, how he had spent all of his adult life without crying and now the tears came so easily. His eyes would moisten at the most mundane of maudlin thoughts that in better times he would have been embarrassed to relate to anybody, least of all his younger brother.

The thought that preoccupied him most nights was this: How much more of this could he take? How many more hurdles would he be able to surmount when each day seemed as if it might be his last. Then there was another thought, one that befuddled him completely: How many days were they from the rapids anyway? Twenty? Twenty-five? A lifetime of days? And most perplexing of all: How many days, weeks, months, years, were they away from the fort? There was no way of determining that either. He and Gilbert knew nothing except that there seemed to be no physical escape from their prison of ice and snow.

No physical escape, but as they plodded on, Will escaped more and more in his mind. He imagined himself in London on a fine summer morning, with the sun shining and the flowers in full bloom. It was gloriously warm. He had just left the house for work, crossing the bridge as children splashed at the water's edge and laughed with each other. What evocative sounds they were! He stopped and watched for a while and felt so connected to them, it might have been he and Gilbert down there playing. A rope swing hung from the limb of a tree and a child straddled the board tied to the rope's end, pumping himself back and forth on it in great arcs. Will could almost feel the cooling breeze against his face. The children looked so carefree, he nearly wept with joy for them.

He had to get to work. Reluctantly, he left the bridge and the children behind and entered the town. Down the boardwalks he strode, his boots resounding against the wood, waving and nodding hello to customers, merchants and others of his acquaintance. It seemed he knew everybody on this day. A breeze that smelled faintly of the land came out of the west and blew away the smell of the brewery, fresh as the morning. Reaching his shop, he realized how much he had enjoyed this wonderful place over the years. What a fool he was even to think of leaving it! The welcome aroma of leather greeted him as he opened the door and it felt so good to be back. How could he have ever felt adrift in a place that was so firmly anchored? Suddenly, his head began to spin and he thought he might swoon. He lost his balance, staggered a bit, then fell heavily to the floor, which was mysteriously covered in snow. When he came to his senses, Gilbert was shaking him, and he could not believe where he was.

Yet at other times, the memories of home and his mother were so vague that they lacked any connection to his present existence. They were like dreams, hard to recall because they existed on a different plane. It was as if the river and this boundless wilderness dominated his past entirely, as if he had been born here, had grown up here and, in all likelihood, would die here.

And just as the river was always there, so was hunger. There was no way to deny or not acknowledge its existence; it wailed inside him like a demanding child and would not be appeased. There were times when he could have gnawed the bark from the trees, and he had no idea what kept him from doing exactly that. He had even thought that if Gilbert died he would seriously consider eating him. He wanted to broach the subject with his brother but could not summon the audacity to do it.

They were above the river now, not more than a dozen feet or so and the land was mercifully flat. Had there been a hill to climb, he doubted that he could do it. The snow here was as powdery as fine sand, and the wind blew the tops of the drifts off in whirling snow devils. Each step was a search for firm footing. A wrong one could easily break a leg and that would be a death warrant. If that happened, he was determined to beg Gilbert to put a bullet through his brain to end his misery.

His lips were chapped raw and his nose ran constantly, the thin mucous freezing in his moustache. He had to keep breaking it away as it built up so that it would not interfere with his breathing. His lower legs felt as if he had immersed them in a hot bath and he did not think that was a good sign. That night, when he and Gilbert were folded into one another beneath their blankets, and he had put his arm around his brother's arms and chest, he felt profoundly serene. It was good to hold his brother close, good to have him so *near*. Only a crazy man would ever want to be alone out here, and Gilbert was the only thing that kept him from going stark raving mad. He held his brother tighter and uttered words that he never imagined would ever pass his lips: "I love you, Gilbert," he said. "I love you." Gilbert said nothing, but a shudder rippled through his body and Will knew that he was not capable of responding, that he, like his older brother, was clinging to the last vestiges of sanity.

In the morning, Will's right foot was numb with frostbite and the left was not far behind. Gilbert had to help him to his feet and the brothers, leaning against each other, moved forward. The snow blew thick upon them all that day, and the next and the next. The river, which had flowed in broad curves for a while, now had sharp bends in it, sometimes flowing as much as two miles east before turning tightly back in the opposite direction for a similar distance. Each bend looked the same as the last, and it seemed as if they were going nowhere. And just as vexing was the fact that since they had left the rapids behind, the river had been as smooth as a lake. They would have sailed through in no time at all had they only been able to get past the ice jam.

Chance could be such a cruel master, Will thought. He could go back in his mind and count the events that led them to this place on the river: the ice jam, the rock, the canyon, spending too long at Tete Jaune Cache, and so on, each event both a cause and an effect. He sometimes wondered if the real reason they had dallied at the Cache was not that they were optimistic about making good time on the river but that they were afraid of it. If only they had done things differently from the very beginning, it might have made all the difference. *If, if, if,* a long line of them at the end of which was he himself, the procrastinator, the dilly-dallier, the man who thought they had all the time in the world. It was his fault they were here in this place at this time and no one else's. He recalled his conversation with Wright back at Fort Garry when he suggested to him that he could turn back. They should have all turned back. None of them had any right being here.

They passed some elongated islands that seemed to split the river in two and late in the afternoon, after they had managed about two miles, came to another sharp bend that sent the river in an easterly direction again. There seemed to be a consistent pattern to these "s" bends, which made it very tempting to strike inland while maintaining a southerly course. But what if this was the last of the bends and river did not come the same distance back? The forest would become their graveyard. Yet the river did return west, even farther than it had gone east.

Will did not know what he noticed first: the swirls in the water that suggested an estuary, or the fort, perched on a bluff a short distance downriver. Whichever it was, the sight initially made no impression on him, so lost was he in reverie. Then he thought that his eyes were playing tricks on him again, that this was a northland equivalent of a desert mirage, forced into his mind by his tormented body. He rubbed his eyes with the back of his wrists, squinted and looked again. It *was* the fort, by God! He could see smoke curling up from a stone chimney, could smell it on the wind. Gilbert saw it, too, and shouted something unintelligible, more like an animal sound than anything human.

Tears filled Will's eyes and he was giddy with relief. For so long he had felt a hair's breadth away from death, and now life lay waiting for him in the guise of a Hudson's Bay Company fort. He wanted to shout with joy but he had no voice; he wanted to dance in celebration but his legs would not allow it. There was such a profound weariness in him that he sagged against Gilbert, who leaned in against him. They looked at each other and he saw tears welling up in his brother's eyes. He wanted to smile but could not do that either. All he could do was feel his own tears freezing on his cheeks.

The estuary was broad and impossible to cross without a boat. Oh, for the wings of an angel, Will thought, that would let them fly to the other side. He felt light enough to do it, and that was a fact. Then Gilbert spotted a canoe tied up on the far bank, and even though it was inaccessible, the hands of men had made it and there was comfort in that knowledge.

They had three shells left between them and decided that they would be best used trying to attract someone's attention. Will's only concern was the wind, which was strong in their faces and might blow the sound of the gunfire away. With stiff fingers, he loaded the Henry, and fired a shot in the air. He waited a few moments, and when he saw no movement around the fort, fired another. He and Gilbert began yelling, croaking really, and waving and still no one came. Frustration rose like bile in them and grew into a sense of utter helplessness. All they could do was save their last shot until someone came out of the fort.

But no one came out. Will's heart felt as clogged with ice as the river. Why this cruelty piled on top of so many others? What was it his mother used to say? Enough is enough and too much is plenty.

Darkness fell and the brothers retreated into the bushes to spend another interminable night huddled together beneath their blankets, this one made even longer by the knowledge that daylight might bring a reprieve from a sentence of death. Excited, Will slept fitfully, and the first thing that entered his mind each time he awoke was that he had no feeling in his feet. He feared losing them. Then, for the first time in what seemed like ages, he thought of Thomas and the others. They also had frozen appendages, and had for far too long now, unless they had been able to thaw them out by the fire. If they still had a fire. If they were still alive.

Gilbert also had trouble sleeping. The best the brothers could do through the long night was try to comfort each other, and even that proved difficult. They were both awake as the grey light of dawn nudged away the darkness, their eyes anxiously glued to the fort. It may have been minutes or perhaps hours — Will could not tell — before a small figure appeared from behind the palisade, wrapped in a shawl. He thought it might be a woman. He had his rifle ready and fired off the last shell, then he and Gilbert began yelling and waving again. Thank God, the wind had died. The person looked their way, waved back, and disappeared inside the fort. Soon a single man came down the slope and along the Fraser's shore toward them. He was an Indian, but the brothers could not have cared less. The sight of another human being, regardless of his race, was an affirmation that they would live to see another day and perhaps, with good fortune, many more. The brothers looked into each other's eyes, sunk deeply in grim, emaciated faces behind straggly, ice-encrusted beards. Their skeletal frames, draped in ragged clothes, were apparitions of their former selves, scarcely recognizable to one another.

On the far side of the Nechako, the Indian untied the canoe and stroked expertly toward them, an angel of mercy cloaked in wolf skin. It was not until the vessel bumped against the shore that the knot that was Will's stomach untied itself.

CHAPTER ELEVEN

FORT GEORGE, DECEMBER 1862–JANUARY 1863

It was late, and though Gilbert was already in bed, Will did not feel like turning in. He had been restless ever since arriving safely at the fort, and worried about Thomas and the others. Coming down the river, he had not had time to give them much thought but now they were on his mind constantly. He figured that Thomas, with his great energy and optimism, stood the best chance to survive and Wright the least. He did not know what to think about Helstone. After all this time, he was not convinced that he knew the man very well. Then again, how much do you ever know about any man? All men kept a part of themselves hidden from view.

Now that it seemed clear no one was going to effect a rescue, at least not for a while, Will was disconsolate. He envied Gilbert, who seemed able to compartmentalize his thoughts and had little or no trouble sleeping, even though he admitted to being upset. Perhaps it was one of those cruel tricks of life, Will thought. He got their mother's looks and Gilbert got her strengths.

They had now been at the fort for more than six weeks, having reached it on December 1. It had taken them four weeks to make the journey down from the rapids, the four most horrific weeks in their lives. (He did not like to think how those same four weeks might have passed for Thomas, Helstone and Wright.) They had arrived scarcely alive, his right foot badly frostbitten, his left less so. Even seeing their weakened condition, Thomas Charles, the fort's manager, had callously declared, "God in heaven, man, it can't be more than 40 miles to those rapids!" as if a child could have done it in no time. The comment did nothing to bolster Will's self-esteem, which had slipped down around his boot tops.

Charles was "country-born," as the saying went, with a Cree mother and a Scots father. He was a burly, erect man of medium height with thick, tar-black hair, grey-streaked, and long sideburns. His dark eyes were watery with a network of veins. He had started out with the Company 30 years before as a common labourer, and through diligence and hard work — along with a fist that clutched a penny as tightly as it did a dollar — he had swiftly climbed the Company ladder. He became a guide and interpreter, and then a clerk, the lowest of the officer ranks and the first at which one could be appointed manager in charge of a post. Such appointments were always to small posts, of course, and Fort George fell into this category. (Though called a fort, technically, Fort George was merely a fur-trading post, and a minor one at that. Several buildings, including a warehouse where the furs were stored, a store in which the business of trading was conducted, two long men's houses and an officer's dwelling where Charles both lived and had an office, were all surrounded by a six-foot palisade designed more for defining a property than for defence.) Small or not, it was as good as a castle to Charles and his demeanour never let anyone doubt who was king. Will guessed he was near 50, but he looked much older, probably due to easy access to the brandy and rum casks.

There was rarely much sympathy emanating from the manager's heart; indeed, he had proved from the outset to be a most unwelcoming host. The fact that two strangers had interrupted the quiet routine of his winter, and brought with them an emergency to boot, appeared to make him surly. But the brothers soon discovered that Charles was surly with everyone except the Indians, with whom he was merely patronizing. He rarely bothered to keep from his voice the disdain that he felt for his surprise guests. "You should have stayed home, sir," he had said to Will on one occasion, as if he thought the brothers were the world's greatest fools. "This country has greenhorns enough without the two of you adding to the numbers." Will could not help but think that perhaps his host was right on both accounts. Nevertheless, on the day the brothers had arrived at the fort Charles had brought them into his quarters to have an employee with some medical experience look at Will's feet. He had sent a servant to summon James Griffin from the store.

"His nefarious past notwithstanding," Charles had told them, "Mr. Griffin is the nearest thing to a doctor that we can muster in this part of the world. He claims that he spent some time in Glasgow studying medicine, but I suspect that he spent most of his time emptying gin bottles and cavorting with Scotch whores. Nevertheless, he has seen a few cases similar to yours, so your life shouldn't be at risk."

Charles had poured the brothers a tot of brandy each and after eyeing them up and down, shook his head, laughed derisively, and added, "You're lucky to be alive."

Will knew that they must have looked hideous to the manager and that they probably smelled disgusting too, but he did not care. For in spite of his condition, a marvellous sense of well-being was washing through him. He was grateful to be alive and glad to be among other human beings again. In fact, just being inside the safety of a house after so many months in the outdoors made him supremely happy. Even better, he was not shivering from the arctic cold anymore! Instead, he was sweating just sitting there. Without even lifting a finger, he felt perspiration oozing from his forehead and rolling down his temples to be trapped in his beard. The warmth surrounded him like a cocoon, and the exquisite comfort and outrageous pleasure of it, combined with the slight smell of wood and tobacco smoke in the air, seemed almost decadent. Nevertheless, he revelled in it. Better decadence than that frozen Hell outside. He did not wish to be back there, not for all the gold in Cariboo. Not now at any rate. He could even smell food cooking, though he could not tell what it was, and his mouth watered so badly that he thought he might drool. Looking back on that first day and that room, and the phenomenal sensations it produced, he might have been in heaven.

"This is good French brandy," Charles had pointed out, as if he might be wasting it on the brothers. "Not the English variety which is merely gin with a tincture of iodine for colour." He had paused and eyed both men before adding, "Not that anyone in your condition should care a whit."

Mrs. Charles, a full-blooded Indian, had come into the room, served the drinks and departed as quickly as she had arrived. She was much younger than the manager and Will had not found her as attractive as the country-born and native women at Fort Edmonton. But a man staying on in this country needed female companionship and that usually meant native. Some, like Charles, even married them.

The strong spirits had put much-needed colour into the brothers' pale cheeks. It had produced a most delicious feeling going down Will's gullet, and made him sweat even more. He felt dizzy from the drink's strength, as if he were going to lose his balance. The chair he was sitting on suddenly seemed as narrow as a fence rail. Charles had tossed his drink back in a single swallow and said, "I will attempt to have two Indians leave for upriver this afternoon or first thing tomorrow morning. If your companions are still alive, they will find them."

Griffin had arrived then, a tall man of kindly disposition and indeterminate age, with the dark, curly hair of a young man and the lined face of someone much older. Jagged streaks of red and blue veins ran down both sides of his nose and scarlet blotches adorned his cheeks. He had treated Will's foot by placing it in the warm water Mrs. Charles had fetched from the kitchen, which felt as if it were scalding. The pain was slow in coming at first, but when it arrived, it did so with an intensity that Will had never before experienced. All that had kept him from crying out was the company of other men and the generous drafts of brandy. "Think pleasant thoughts," Griffin had said, then pricked the blisters with a sewing needle and rubbed salve on them. Will thought of the party back at Fort Edmonton, spoke of it, thinking that it would help, but despite the colourful images and the numbness from the liquor, he had wanted to scream. Afterward Griffin had wrapped the foot in a cloth. "That should do you," he told Will, "although you won't be dancing for a while."

After Griffin had departed, Mrs. Charles brought in a plate of boiled turnips for each of the brothers. "Easy does it, lads," Charles had said. "You'll fare better if you eat just a little bit at a time." But the brothers had not been able to help themselves and ignored the caution, wolfing down the food. How exquisite it had been, Will remembered, to feel it slide down his throat and into a stomach that had been empty for so long. But later, he had paid for his gluttony. A pain had grown in his gut that rose into his chest, as though someone had set it on fire. Then he threw it all up. Gilbert, too, had been in pain, but had managed to keep his meal down.

They were out of food and had been for three or four weeks. Nearly a month since they ate the beaver tails, which was a month after Will and Gilbert had left for Fort George. It was probably getting close to Christmas or perhaps even past it already. Talk about rescue had dried up like rain pools in the desert. It was now simply a case of how long they could survive, how long before they wasted away to skin and bones and then to nothing.

In their weakened condition, it had become too much of a struggle to gather firewood: They did not have the strength to swing the hatchet or carry the wood back to camp. The great pile that had been left for them, which they had supplemented, had dwindled to a small mound. When that was gone, so was the fire. Sometimes, he found it too burdensome to muster enough strength to care.

He had moments when lethargy nearly overwhelmed him and he was tempted to give up, to let go and slip away from all this misery. But just when it seemed that would be an easy thing to do, something clicked on inside him and he could not do it. It just was not in him to let go. Not yet anyway. He still had many years left in him. He wanted to live.

Charles had shown the brothers to their quarters and they slept through the remainder of the day and night. Both had awakened stiff and sore, but eager to find out if the manager had kept his word. He had, having dispatched two Indians that very morning to try to locate the stranded party.

"There are no guarantees that they will get through in this weather," he had said. It had begun to snow again. "Indeed, I will be surprised if they do."

"We are in your debt, sir," Will told him, and Charles's bearing had indicated that he agreed. However, two days later, the Indians had returned. The snow was too deep, they complained. Worse, the wind had picked up and reduced visibility to only a few yards. All they could do was wait and hope that the weather would improve. But it had not and remained nasty over the next few days, limiting movement everywhere.

The brothers were quartered with Griffin in the men's house, one of two that were used for company employees of lower rank and visitors of common stature. The rectangular buildings faced each other across the compound, each containing four sets of three rooms. A set included a main room-cum-kitchen with a rough-hewn table and chairs and a cot against one wall, and two bedrooms. Will and Gilbert shared one bedroom while the rum-reeking James Griffin occupied the other. The window "glass" was merely moosehide stretched thinly over the opening to keep the cold air out and let a minimum of light in. Ice easily built up along the sill, but the rooms were reasonably warm. A large fireplace dominated the centre of the rooms, its hearth facing the main room and a half of its back in each of the tiny bedrooms. An ingenious structure, typical of how local products were put to good use in this far country, it was built of stone plastered over with a mixture of horse manure, clay, straw and lime. Bits of straw stuck out through the plaster, here and there. It was not much to look at, but a fire burning all day would warm the plaster and radiate heat into all three rooms long after it went out.

There were two cots in the brothers' room, both made from small logs with straw mattresses on rope springs that sagged badly in the middle. It was a drastic change after sleeping on the hard ground for so long, and Will felt arthritic when he arose the following morning. "Sleep tight," his mother would say to him, always making sure the ropes were kept tight on the beds at home, "and you'll feel much the better for it in the morning." Nevertheless, he was glad to have a bed to sleep in, regardless of how badly it sagged. After all, he was alive and in tolerably good health again, and scarcely a day went by that he did not count his blessings.

Now their ordeal seemed distant and reduced to bits and pieces, like a half-remembered nightmare. They had been gone from home seven months — six months of that travel just to get this far — and had still not reached their goal. And he had believed it would take only six to eight weeks! Charles was right. What bloody fools they were! If they had had any sense at all, they would have spent the money and taken the steamer out of New York. In all probability, they would have been mining for gold before the summer was out.

Anyhow, Will was making a slow recovery. His feet were healing daily, although his right foot still troubled him to walk on. He and Gilbert were doing their level best to work for their bed and board, mostly bucking and chopping wood to keep the many hearths in the fort supplied.

Christmas came and Charles celebrated the season with free rations of rum for the men and a meal that featured small cuts of lynx and rabbit. When Charles informed the Rennies of the celebration and that they were invited, he said it as if the entire affair was a waste of his time and the Company's money.

It was the first time that Will had seen the entire layout of the building that housed Charles and his wife and in which the manager had his office. Built from sawn timber, it had multi-paned glass windows and a porch that wrapped around two sides. As one entered the front door, the manager's office was to the left and a bedroom for visitors of high rank to the right. Down the hall on the same side was a parlour opposite which was the couple's bedroom. (Will had managed a peek, and the room appeared big enough to contain the three rooms he and Gilbert shared with Griffin.) Farther along was a short hallway branching off to a spacious dining room that had been added to the main building. Beyond that was the back entrance to the dwelling and a freestanding, covered breezeway that led to the kitchen.

Ropes were hung on pegs in the breezeway and someone had explained to Will that they were there to pull the sturdy log structure out from between the residence and the kitchen in case of a fire. Since fires nearly always broke out in the kitchen and destroyed it, this saved having to rebuild the residence as well. Will thought this extremely practical, just as he did the dried and stiff snakeskins that lay on the floor by the walls. He had asked Charles their purpose. "They are rattlesnake skins," he replied, "brought up from Fort Kamloops. Though I find snakes disgusting creatures in general, their skins are very useful. The smell of them keeps the mice population at bay."

The New Year arrived on the back of a fierce storm that disappeared by late morning, leaving behind a stiff wind and blue skies. The temperature plummeted even further. Gilbert could see the anguish etched in his brother's face and, wanting to ease it, suggested that perhaps Charles was the wrong man to ask for help. There was a Negro trapper wintering in a cabin not far from the fort who seemed a very resourceful individual. He came into the fort's store with furs from time to time. Maybe if the brothers paid him a visit he could offer some constructive help.

They walked down to the cabin, Will limping on his painful feet and struggling to get through the snow, though Gilbert broke a trail for him. It was only a quarter-mile from the fort, but the effort nearly wore him out. A bearded black man of medium height answered their knock on the cabin door and the brothers introduced themselves.

Giscome was a native of Jamaica. Though born a slave to an English master, he had no memories of it for he was just three years old when the British finally abolished trade in human beings. A restless man, he had left the island in his early 20s, bound for the goldfields of California where he prospected for several years with only limited success. Eventually, the tough racist laws of the state drove him out. He and a few hundred other blacks moved north to British Columbia at the invitation of none other than Governor James Douglas himself. Many stayed in Victoria and started businesses, but Giscome was a prospector and hoped one day to find the motherlode. Meanwhile, he eked out a living as a trapper.

The brothers explained their reason for paying him a visit. Giscome knew the story, of course, as did everyone who had visited the fort, but could offer no suggestions.

"I wish I could help you," he said, his deep and powerful voice that of a much larger man. He spoke with a heavy Caribbean accent, but his command of English was flawless. "I've not been to the area of which you speak, although I plan to go there come spring. That might be a little late for your purposes, though. The only people who could conceivably reach there at this time of year would be the Indians, and it would be difficult enough even for them. I know several of them well, though, and would not hesitate to ask for you."

He offered the brothers tea, which they accepted. It must have been steeping on the stove for a long time for it was strong and bitter. The men lit pipes as they sipped the hot brew. Giscome was telling them of some of his past exploits when the door swung open, startling all three men. In came four Indians as if it were their home, filling the cabin with a blast of cold air and the smell of rancid fish. The howling wind had hidden the sound of their approach. The Rennies were alarmed until they saw a smile of recognition flash across Giscome's face. The trapper knew the visitors and spoke to them in French, some of which Will understood. They had come from their village in the north, they said, news that quickened his heart. With his rudimentary French, he formed two questions in his mind before he spoke and could not get them out fast enough. "Did you come through the rapids many miles up the river? Did you see any white men?"

They did not understand him. He spoke the questions in English to Giscome, who translated. Will could not tell from the Indians' demeanour if they were answering yes or no. Giscome told him, "They came from the north, but they used a different route."

"Ask them if they'll be returning to their village via the river." Will felt a spark of excitement.

Giscome asked, "*Retournez-vous au village par la rivière?*"

"*Non. C'est trop difficile et ça prend trop de temps.*"

Giscome looked at Will and shook his head. "They won't," he said. "It's a much longer and harder journey."

Another carrot of hope dangled in front of them, cruelly snatched away. The brothers finished their tea, thanked Giscome for his hospitality and left for the fort. Will felt completely frustrated.

Chapter Twelve

January 18, 1863

"My Dear Mother,

I have stayed awake for nights trying to think of a good way to start this letter but can think of none. Our Thomas is gone, as are John Helstone and John Wright, all victims of this terrible country.

"Gilbert and I arrived at Fort George several weeks ago in a terrible condition after one of the roughest journeys any poor mortal has had in the world. We got stuck on a rock in a rapid in the Fraser River, more than 50 miles from here, and could not get off. This happened at the end of October. (You should know, Mother, that the Fraser River is nothing like the River Thames. It is wide and deep and full of fierce rapids, which turned out to be too much for us to handle.)

"It snowed and froze most desperately. Thomas and both Johns, Helstone and Wright, had their hands and feet frozen and so dispatched Gilbert and me to the fort for provisions and assistance. The snow was so deep and travelling through the woods so laborious, it took us 28 days to accomplish the task. We had only one meal of provisions and for the last two weeks of our journey had not a single bite to eat. I froze my feet so badly, and was so weak by the time we reached the side of the river opposite to the fort, I had to be carried to the canoe. (You must not worry, Mother, for I am all but mended.)

"Though we expended every effort, we could get no one at the fort to go to Thomas's assistance. They said there was too much snow and the river was not frozen hard enough for safe travel. The Indians could probably get through now, but they are no longer interested. We have no money so there is nothing in it for them. Had Gilbert and I been capable of the return trip, we would have gone in an instant.

"We left them all of our provisions, which amounted to only a 10-day supply of food. That means they have been out of food now for two months which, combined with endless days of severe weather, leaves little doubt as to their fate. I am deeply sorry that I have placed the added burden of notifying Mssrs. Helstone's and Wright's loved ones squarely upon your shoulders in the midst of your own bereavement, but it would be best if they heard it directly from you rather than through the impersonal nature of a letter.

"During my restless nights, I have thought of Thomas, you and home often. Do you remember when he was just eight and he broke through the ice while we were skating? He was so cold, yet he never once complained. It was the same on the Fraser, Mother. We were all soaked and frozen by the time we got to shore after being stranded on the rock, but Thomas never once complained. You would have been as proud of him as was I.

"The good news is that Gilbert came through our adventure in relatively good health, although he's much thinner than you will remember him to be. (We both are, in fact.) He sends his love, and, like me, would give anything to be with you during a time when you will surely need us most.

"I wish I had better news to tell you about Fort George. It is barely a small patch of civilization in this vast wilderness, and Mr. Charles, the manager, is most inhospitable. He has stated his wishes clearly, that he does not want us to stay any longer than we absolutely have to and that we should go as soon as I'm well enough to travel. The reason he gives is that he does not have enough provisions to feed two more mouths over the winter. I can't say if it is true — he will not allow us in the cache house where the winter provisions are stored — but Mr. Charles is lord over all he surveys and we, as his subordinates, have little choice but to do his bidding. I do not know what the conditions are like between here and Quesnellemouth this time of year, but Mr. Charles says the trail is well travelled by fur brigades.

"I fear that you will think this entire episode is my fault, that if we had left London a month earlier, as Thomas wanted, none of this would have happened. Please believe me when I say that it was simply a case of bad luck. Had we not run up on the rock, we would have sailed safely to Fort George, for the river below the rapids was smooth and safe all the way. Still, I must confess to moments when I feel that the responsibility is indeed mine and mine alone. During these moments, I cannot help but feel unworthy to be your son. Should you feel similarly, then I beg your forgiveness.

Your affectionate son,
William"

He had dreaded having to write this letter but felt better now that it was done. Even so, he had left out many things, particularly Carpenter's death. There was no need to include that horrific episode. (He had already written a letter to James Carpenter's wife in Toronto, briefly outlining the accident. He wanted to send the diary too, but feared it would get lost in the mail, which could be unreliable. He would have to find another way of getting it to her.) Folding the paper, he wrote the address on it, then took the candle from its holder on the table and dripped wax over the edge to seal it, quickly, before he changed his mind about the some of the things he had said, difficult things written behind a buffer of 2,500 miles that could never be said face to face. Once the wax had hardened, he took his pen once more and edged the letter in black, so that his mother would have some warning about its contents. Then he put it in his jacket pocket. He did not know when the next courier to Fort St. James and the coast was leaving, but he would ensure the letter went with him.

Will and Gilbert had gone to see Charles in the officer's dwelling house the previous night, at his behest. Will rarely felt comfortable going there because it reminded him of Eldon House back in London. Not that they were similarly constructed; rather, it was what they represented: Both had ways of letting him know that he was only a shoemaker.

The brothers entered the building and knocked on the door to Charles's office, which was closed to keep in the heat. The manager called "Enter" and they went in. A fire crackled and sparked in the hearth and a few long candles lit up the sparsely furnished room, which included a hutched desk in a corner and a few chairs around a small table in the centre. A picture of Queen Victoria and a framed HBC coat-of-arms hung on the wall. Charles was at his desk, which faced into the corner, pen in hand, writing the daily entry in the Company logbook. He turned around as the brothers entered and motioned them to chairs around the table, then came and joined them.

A bottle of rum sat on the table alongside three glasses. Charles poured a tot for each of them, giving himself twice the amount he gave the Rennies. The men lit pipes and tobacco smoke curled thickly about their heads. The meeting had all the earmarks of heading in a convivial direction, but Will understood Charles well enough to know that such a course was unlikely. Indeed, he had recognized instinctively what the meeting was about upon receiving the summons, and that he and Gilbert, like pigs, were merely being fattened for the slaughter. To put off the inevitable, he told the manager about their visit with John Giscome and the arrival of the Indians.

"They had come from a village up north," he said. "But when I asked, they said that they hadn't come by the rapids, nor had they seen any white men. Gilbert and I had hoped that they might return home along the river but they said no. It was too hard and too long."

Charles tugged at his beard with a hand as mottled as a trout's back. "Humph. That may be what they told you," he said, "but it isn't necessarily what they'll do. They now know that there's a white man's camp up the river and that in all likelihood its inhabitants are dead. That means there will be bounty for the taking: clothes and various and sundry other things, most importantly weapons. That is, if they haven't been beaten to it by someone else. What they'll like best of all is that it won't cost them a single fur. I wouldn't be surprised, were I you, if they've not already been there."

"And if our brother and our friends were still alive?"

"You shouldn't assume that. I don't think that it's even remotely possible. But should I be proven wrong, there is no reason to believe that the Indians would do them any harm. These are Carrier Indians with little taste for blood. What they would probably do is help them with one hand and rob them with the other. Your own experience should tell you that the land itself is the enemy here, not the Indians." He drew on his pipe before continuing, letting out a long stream of smoke as he spoke. "This is no less true for the Company than for anybody else. If white men are to survive in this wilderness, it will only be with the Indians' help and co-operation. They understand its whims far better than we do. Unless you've lost most of your senses, you'll know by now that their worst feature is their unequalled filthiness. They stink worse than the pair of you did when you first arrived, and if they ran out of food, they could feast on the lice and fleas that they carry — which they sometimes do anyway. It's too bad. A few civilized baths and they would be as tolerable as you or I. What is probably impossible to correct is that they can be a shiftless lot when there is nothing in it for them." Charles sighed as if he alone bore the onerous weight of this perceived character flaw.

Will wanted to say that the same thing might apply to the Company, but refrained. It seemed to him that the manager thought the Company was hard done by. But Will had been in the warehouse and seen the variety of skins hanging from the rafters: coyote, ermine, fisher, mink, fox of different varieties, lynx, beaver and otter. There were so many of them he was amazed that he and Gilbert had seen so few animals on their way down the river. On the other hand, perhaps that was the reason why they had not seen many animals: they were being over-trapped. Whatever was happening, the Company did not appear to be suffering.

Charles took another draft of rum and said, "But I didn't bring you here to discuss Indians, except to say that they apparently are not the least bit interested in your problem. You are here because of my need to impress upon you that you cannot stay any longer. We have neither the food nor the room for you, so you must move on as quickly as possible."

Charles's bluntness did not surprise Will, for he usually spoke to the brothers as a superior to his underlings. "We will pay for the

Company's services, sir," Will said. "We have nothing to trade, except perhaps our firearms, nor have we any money, but rest assured that we will send some to you once we do. You have our word on it."

Charles shook his head. "It has nothing to do with money, Mr. Rennie. Perhaps under normal circumstances your board might be feasible, but we have employees who need feeding through the winter and our provisions are seriously low. A large contingent of would-be miners from the east passed through here in October, and they were only slightly better off than you. Their leader was a schoolmaster named McMicking." He shook his head and laughed derisively. "A schoolmaster as ill-equipped to face this land as you two. It's odd how the thought of gold can turn a seemingly rational man into a fool prepared to take such risks. They had lost men, too, some to the river and one to diphtheria. A young man not 20 years old. They buried him just outside the walls of this fort. They also reduced our food supply to barely tolerable levels, particularly with winter about to set in. There were thieves among them, too, if the low yield of turnips from our garden was any indication. My point is, gentlemen, neither money nor articles of trade can obtain what we do not have. So when you leave, I would advise you to stay off the river — there are two sets of dangerous rapids between here and Quesnellemouth and, given your experience, I'm sure you would rather avoid them. The trail south is well established and used by fur brigades quite regularly, so you won't need a guide. It's less than a hundred miles to the mouth, and you should reach it easily."

"I'm afraid my feet are not healed well enough to make such a walk," Will said. "Perhaps the Indians can carry me there on a palanquin like some Eastern rajah."

Charles ignored the sarcasm. "There is much improvement in your feet," he said. "Your limp has all but disappeared."

"That might be true for short distances and around the fort, but long distances are another matter. It doesn't take much to set my feet to aching."

This was not entirely the case. The truth of the matter was that Will had mixed feelings about going. Despite the less-than-hospitable atmosphere at the fort, it was at least a safe haven. Beyond its walls lay more miles of the unknown and, worst of all, the dreadful cold. He did not feel up to the challenge of facing either just yet.

"I will need a few more days," he said. "Perhaps a week. But you can be sure that we will take our leave at the first opportunity. We would not want to impose on you and the Company any more than we have already." Will said this in as polite a tone as he could muster, hoping that the contempt he felt for Charles had not risen to the surface.

"I am a generous man," said Charles. "I will give you a fortnight. Then you must be gone."

The brothers stood up to leave, nodding curtly.

Charles stood, too, so that he was not looking up. "One more thing before you go," he said. "You will need food for the journey. That is obvious, and the only place you can get it is here." He looked directly at Will. "I will accept your Henry as payment." He turned his back to the brothers and strode to his desk, signalling with a wave of his hand that they were dismissed.

Will was livid. His Henry in trade? He had no doubt as to who would reap the benefits of that transaction, and it would not be the Company. A reckless part of him wanted to strike out at Charles or, at the very least, to leave first thing in the morning and show the manager that they needed neither him nor the

Company. But there was more to it than that. Regardless of his reservations about continuing their journey, Will also felt that he and Gilbert had not put enough effort toward getting up a rescue party for Thomas and the others, even though they had practically begged Charles on several occasions to send someone north. The manager's story, however, was invariably the same: Conditions would not allow it. The fact that it was beyond Will's control did nothing to assuage his guilt.

His companions were not coping very well with their ordeal; otherwise, why would they be so perturbed that he spent most of the daylight hours immersed in his Bible? He told them, "Never have its words meant so much to me; they are my food, my succor." Reading aloud invigorated him. He said that the words revealed to him that they were all sinners, most particularly himself. After all, why else they would they be placed in this perilous predicament? Surely, this must be God's way of punishing them. Yet there was no reason to think that salvation was not available to them. He could see a path leading straight to it, a path running directly through him. He was the link to their redeemer. Through him, their sins would be cast out and they would all find salvation. Through him, they could hear and pay heed to the Bible's important words that he knew instinctively were relevant: "I am the bread of life. He that cometh to me shall never hunger; and he that believeth in me shall never thirst."

So he read long passages out loud and even committed to memory the gist of those he deemed especially relevant so that he could recite them after dark, those

that he was positive his companions needed to hear and
to contemplate, utterly convinced that they would be
benefited in their time of need. The passion he felt during
these moments lifted his spirits, and yet sometimes he
felt as if he were teetering on the edge of a great abyss
and that one small slip would send him hurtling into a
nightmare worse than the one that was his daily existence.

The brothers stomped along the boardwalk, between banks of
shovelled snow, back to their quarters. Griffin was sitting at the
table with a glass of rum.

"I could hear you coming," he said. "I take it your meeting did
not go well."

Will described the affair. Griffin merely smiled and said, "There is
an air about Mr. Charles that is uncommonly easy to dislike."

The brothers sequestered themselves in their room. Will expressed
his concern about not having done enough to save Thomas and the
others. He and Gilbert had had this discussion before and Gilbert
had already accepted what he deemed was the inevitable: Thomas
was dead.

"You're hoping against hope, Will," he said. "I don't like the shape
of things any better than you do, but you need to ask yourself how
they could have possibly survived for this long."

"I ask myself that every day," Will said, "and I'm unwilling to
accept the answer that everyone else believes so readily."

"That's simply not realistic, Will; it's just that everyone else around
here understands this country a lot better than we do. You know as
well as I what the weather's been like, and their food supply must
have run out two months ago. Maybe they got lucky and shot a
small animal or two, but you know how many we saw on our way
downriver. It was as if the country had been emptied of them. And

they could not have gone into the forest hunting in their condition. They would have had to wait for an animal to stumble into the camp. You know how tough it was for us."

"But look what we did in two weeks without any food whatsoever."

"We were lucky."

"Maybe they will be too. Surely there's at least an outside chance that some friendly Indians happened by and either left them food or took them to their village."

Gilbert shook his head. "Indians come to the fort all the time, and if that had happened, don't you think we would have heard about it by now?"

"Then maybe a deer or moose wandered by the camp. You don't know." Will recognized that he was clutching at straws, but what else was there to do? He loathed the thought of having to write his mother with news that her youngest son was dead, especially when he was having such a hard time believing it himself.

Gilbert sighed. "Well, the only people capable of making the trip are the Indians, and they won't go, will they? And if they won't go, who will? Us? We only made it here by the grace of God. We'd be bloody fools to try a second time, and I'm not prepared to take the risk. I'm worried enough about going south on the brigade trail this time of year."

"You're giving up too easily, Gilbert."

"No. You're hanging on too hard, Will. You need to let go. You are not responsible for this mess."

But he felt that he was. And to let go was to admit that Thomas, Wright and Helstone were lost to them forever. To let go was to lose the last shred of hope, beyond which lay nothing but grief. And he was as much afraid of that as he was of anything.

Though he was not tired, he told Gilbert that he was and wanted to turn in. Truthfully, he had only grown weary of arguing and needed to be alone with his thoughts. He lay awake until long after Gilbert had retired and had started to snore softly, listening to the sounds of the cabin creaking in the cold and thinking. He tossed from one side to the other well into the early hours of the morning, unable to find comfort and not knowing which hurt more, his feet or his heart. He thought how Thomas had probably saved his life back at the rapids, when the canoe had been struck by a block of ice and capsized. And he remembered, many years back, skating on the River Thames with Thomas when his brother was only seven or eight, the same year that Louisa died.

Will had checked the ice and it seemed solid enough, but Thomas hit a thin patch and fell through. Will was horror-stricken. His first instinct was to plunge into the freezing water after his brother, but common sense won out. He raced to the shore and broke off a long branch from an overhanging tree, amazed that he found the strength to do it, then lay on the ice and slithered out to where Thomas was thrashing. He felt the ice crack beneath him, but it held as he thrust the stick at Thomas, who grabbed hold of it. Will backed up, pulling the youngster to safety. That Thomas had shivered all the way home and never once complained impressed Will no end, and though they were opposites and sometimes argued heatedly, he had always respected his brother's courage in the face of adversity.

Was he able to muster a similar courage in the river camp? To what lengths would he go to survive?

Will lay there with such thoughts awhirl in his head. He regretted, too, every harsh word he had ever said to Thomas; they all seemed so childish now. He did not fall asleep until he had at last resigned himself to the hopelessness of Thomas's fate and to his own: that of letting loose the floodgates of grief and writing to his mother the letter that he had been putting off for so long.

CHAPTER THIRTEEN

JANUARY 1863–JANUARY 1864

Will and Gilbert left Fort George for Quesnellemouth on January 26, on their own, without the benefit of an Indian guide. They had with them only the worn clothes on their backs, their blankets and some food. Gilbert had handed over Helstone's shotgun to Thomas Charles for a few pounds of potatoes and Will's precious Henry was equal to 12 smoked salmon. The transaction did not sit well with them but it was beyond their control.

They passed the rapids that Charles had spoken of and shuddered to think of running them in any kind of vessel, let alone a canoe. Six days from the fort, they encountered a Company fur brigade on its way from Fort Alexandria to Fort St. James. By then the brothers had eaten all of the potatoes and had only three salmon left. Since they were only slightly more than halfway to their destination, the brigade leader, who possessed a more generous nature than did Charles, bestowed upon them enough food to see them through to the settlement, which they reached on February 5, in good health, if not good spirits. They had averaged nine miles a day, seven to eight more than they had averaged on their way down from the rapids.

For two weeks, they rested up at a roadhouse and worked off the cost of their room and board by chopping wood and doing other menial chores. People were abuzz with news from the gold creeks of another big strike, this one by miners who had decided to winter there. The news did not affect the brothers as positively as it might have in better circumstances. Both men felt more like going home, and all that kept them from doing so was a lack of money and perhaps the monumental struggle it had taken to get here.

Their first priority was to obtain work for which they would be paid in cold hard cash, and since there was none to be had in Quesnellemouth, they went south. The trail followed the Fraser until it reached a small river that they followed for several miles to Williams Lake. It was the farthest away from the Fraser they had been in months, and Will was glad to see the last of it for a while. Not that he was apt to forget it.

Lately, all they had been doing was sitting around
staring at each other's gaunt faces. Any sign of optimism
that might have been there had long since gone,
faded away like the morning star. They had reconciled
themselves to the stark fact that no one was coming for
them, that this camp would be their graveyard. But he
was determined to survive and knew how to do it, knew
that he had been right all along. The most practical and
available source of food was right here in camp. Still,
the utter clarity of that thought astonished him. He did
not remember when he began to fantasize about killing
someone for food. The idea was suddenly just there and
it was odd how easily it had settled in his mind. Why
wait for someone to die? It simply didn't make any sense

if he was going to survive. There was never any objection from his conscience about these thoughts; he knew straightaway that he could do it, without any qualms. Then the notion grew that if he did not, he himself would be killed. The more he thought about it, the more convinced he was of just such a possibility. And the more imperative it became to act first.

He reasoned that he should get it over with before he was too weak to carry it out. He considered the various ways he might do it, the easiest being using his rifle. But what if it misfired? That would provide an opportunity for retaliation, and in his weakened condition he could easily be overpowered, which might prove fatal. A knife was probably best, deep into a sleeping body. Whatever method he ultimately chose, he wondered why he had taken so long to decide upon the idea.

Will and Gilbert found work at Williams Lake as labourers clearing a path for the new wagon road that would link the coast with Soda Creek. Smallpox was rampant among the Indians in the area, but the big news around this tiny settlement was of a man named John Cameron, the miner who had made the huge strike that the brothers had heard about back in Quesnellemouth. He had come through with the strangest cargo the people here had ever seen: his wife, in a coffin on a sled pulled by a horse. Apparently, she had died from mountain fever, and Cameron was honouring her last request to take her back home to Canada West and bury her there. Will was impressed. Lesser men might have thought it all right just to leave her where she was. After all, she was dead. Cameron was obviously a man of his word with a well-developed sense of loyalty.

The brothers worked hard and saved their money, and when the first miners from the south began trickling through, bound for Williams Creek, they followed. Both were still of a mind to go home but lacked the necessary funds, and the word down from the mines was that even labourers were making good wages. More than that, though, they owed it to Thomas, their mother and themselves to at least see this fabled place.

With most of the snow gone, they reached Quesnellemouth in just a few days. The construction of several new buildings was already underway along the muddy track that fronted the river. They stopped in at Dan McBride's roadhouse where they learned that a man named Peter Skene Ogden had been looking for them. Ogden was an important Company man, in charge of all the forts in the area. The brothers went off immediately to see him, hoping that he might have news of their brother and friends, and not just a demand for payment for their lengthy stay at Fort George.

Ogden was a robust man with grey hair, a strong nose and a pouty lower lip. He had been in the fur-trade business all his life, having started with the Northwest Company, and was, like every other officer of the HBC that Will and Gilbert had met, a man who could swagger sitting down. Probably even more so because of his exalted position. In a very forthright manner, he introduced himself and told the brothers to sit down.

"I am afraid that I have received bad news from Mr. Charles in Fort George. As you may know, his wife is a Carrier Indian and she overheard some of her people saying that they had been to the camp near the rapids where your brother and his companions were isolated. Mr. Charles immediately questioned the Indians. He discovered that they had indeed visited the site and had found everyone there dead. Two of the bodies were under blankets in a shelter while a third lay some distance away, a much older man, they said, than the others. We're sure to find out more as time passes, but right now there just isn't much to go on, except that the Indians buried all three men before they left. Those are the facts as they've come down to me from Mr. Charles."

"When was this discovery made?" asked Will.

"Somewhere around the middle of January, I believe."

Just as he was writing the letter to his mother, Will thought. He wondered if the Indians who found the camp were the same ones he had met at Giscome's cabin. Charles had said that their actions were often contrary to their stated intentions.

The brothers thanked Ogden for the information and left, but as far as Will was concerned, he had raised more questions than he had answered. If blankets covered two bodies, then the one who fled must have been the last to die, and if he was an older man, then it must have been Helstone. How had it come to pass that he outlasted the two younger and stronger men? What was it like for him, with his companions dead and precious little hope that he himself would survive. How did Thomas die? And John Wright? From starvation? Or was it an illness such as pneumonia? And why was Helstone found several yards away? Was he driven mad by loneliness and being in the company of death day in and day out? So mad that he ran off into the forest to put an end to his misery? Was it actually Helstone? What transpired in those last days of human life in that awful place? And the most important and maybe the most unanswerable question of all — the one that truly haunted Will — how long had they been dead?

Those last days must have been a nightmare for all three men. Will wondered how long they had held on to the hope that rescuers would come. For as long as they lived, he supposed, and if there was a merciful God, that would not have been too long.

The brothers worked for more than a month on Williams Creek, mucking for gold at the bottom of a dark and dangerous pit adjacent to Cameron Town, one of four small villages springing up along the creek and named for John Cameron himself. The frenzy of building activity was unlike anything they had ever seen. Yet none of the area's abundant enthusiasm rubbed off on them. They had crossed plains and mountains, forded and sailed rivers, breached countless obstacles thrown across their path to reach a place that Will had thought at times was merely a myth. If, after all that, they were lucky enough to find gold, it would be a bonus, if not anti-climactic. Their bonanza was the hard-won goal of simply being there in the first place.

Pay on the creek was as good as they had heard and they earned $12 a day, which was roughly equivalent to what they earned in a month back home. They worked from dawn until dusk every day except Sunday and soon had more than enough to buy their passage home. Will considered sending money to Fort George for the board he and Gilbert had received, but decided that his Henry was payment enough.

They left Williams Creek on June 17 and made their way to Victoria, another place of enormous activity. On the long road to the coast, they were among the anomalous few going against the robust flow of traffic north. In Victoria, they bought passage on steamers to San Francisco and to Panama, then on to New York. A few connecting trains saw them to Toronto and home.

The pleasures of a long journey were marred by sporadic arguments about Thomas and whether they had done enough to try to save him. Will precipitated these until Gilbert finally told him, directly, that he had said all he was going to say on the subject; in fact, he had said it long ago at Fort George. And as the ships plowed the high seas and the trains steamed across the landscape, an irreparable rift opened between the brothers.

Toronto had experienced stunning growth over the years since Will's last visit. The harbour was jammed with sailing ships at anchor and lined up along the many piers jutting into the water. Front Street was busy with carriages, drays and people behind which the city seemed infinite. After asking directions, they took a horse-car up Yonge Street to Dundas and walked over to Bond Street. Turning north on Bond, sun-filled and tree-lined, they found the address they were looking for, a fashionable brick building of two storeys. Their knock on the door was answered by an attractive young woman dressed in black.

"Mrs. Carpenter?" Will inquired.

"Yes," she replied, a look of suspicion creeping into her face.

Will knew how he and Gilbert must look after weeks of travelling, and quickly introduced himself and his brother. "I wrote you the letter," he said. "I've brought you something."

"Please, come in."

She made them tea and Will told her the full story, how they had met her husband at Fort Edmonton, the benefit he was to the party and his last day on the river. He handed her Carpenter's diary, which she accepted with trembling hands. She turned naturally to the last entry, and her face grew pale as she read the lines there. She closed the book and clutched it to her breast. "Thank you for this," she whispered. "Thank you for this." Two streams of tears flowed over the rose-coloured patches that had formed on her cheeks.

They arrived in London unannounced, precisely the way they wanted it. Though Gilbert was desperate to see Mary and Lucas, he felt he should stop with Will to see their mother. They hired a cabriolet to take them there. Until the carriage wheels clattered over the bridge spanning the Thames, Will had been impatient to be home: The train ride down from Toronto had seemed abominably slow, and so had the cab ride to this point. But now that he was close to facing his mother, he had a sudden urge to prolong the trip, to put the meeting off as long as possible. He could not slow their progress, though, and far too soon they swayed to a stop in front of his home.

Thirteen months had passed since they had left this yard, through the gate on the split-rail fence they had helped their father build. They climbed the short flight of stairs to the front porch. Nothing had changed except themselves. Their mother had seen them through the window and opened the front door just as they reached the top step. She ran to them, thin and gaunt herself, still dressed in black, and fell into their outstretched arms.

The ensuing months were not easy for the brothers, particularly Will, who for the longest time could not look his mother in the eye. But she did not place an ounce of blame on his shoulders and said only, "You cannot hold yourself responsible for events beyond your control. I would not demand that of you. Nor would Thomas."

It was also difficult facing Catherine Helstone and Elizabeth Wright, and through his mother, he had asked for their forgiveness. Both had generously said that there was nothing to forgive. Yet he could not forgive himself.

He and Gilbert had few friendly encounters. Their estrangement upset their mother and added to her grief over the loss of Thomas. She tried to heal the relationship, but the brothers could not find room for peace in their hearts.

Gilbert returned to work at the shoe factory and Will went back to his shop after giving his lessee enough time to relocate. He spent more time in Haystead's public house than he ought to have.

Christmas of 1863 came and went, passed quietly but under strain with Gilbert and his family. The season seemed empty without Thomas.

Will often dreamt of Carpenter and himself in the river, whitewater boiling all around them, Carpenter reaching out a hand to be saved, Will grabbing it only to have it slip through his grasp. Try as he might, he could never save him.

On the anniversary of the brothers' departure from Fort George, Will stopped in at the Emporium to buy a copy of the *London News*. Beside a small stack of the local paper were some copies of Toronto's *Globe* that had just arrived on the afternoon train and, as he sometimes did, Will picked one up. He did not stop at Haystead's that evening and instead went directly home. After dinner, though it generally was not his custom, he helped his mother clean up. She still looked haggard and worn, but she could at least smile now and was adding colour to her previously all-black attire. They took tea into the parlour where they sat and read the newspapers, he the *News* and she the *Globe*. He found little that interested him and happened to glance up at his mother. Her face had gone ashen. "Oh, my God!" she moaned, as the paper fell from her hands on to her lap. She put her hands to her cheeks. "Oh, my God, William! Whatever have we done to deserve this?"

He went to her and took the paper, which she had turned to the second page. At the very top, the story leaped out at him:

> "We reprint here a story from a newspaper in Victoria, in the colony of Vancouver Island, a follow-up to a story printed in these pages last summer concerning the Rennie family of London, C. W. whom, readers may recall, had travelled overland to the western goldfields.
> The *British Colonist*, December 14, 1863.

A Fearful Tragedy

Heartrending Particulars of the Fate of Three Canadians. Revolting Cannibalism.

From Mr. John Giscome, whose interesting narrative of a prospecting tour from the Mouth of Quesnelle to a distance 360 miles east of the Rocky Mountains appears elsewhere, we have the following horrible details of the fate of the portion of a party of Canadians who attempted to cross overland to Cariboo ... "

With all the courage he could muster, Will read on.

Part Four

THE CAMP

CHAPTER FOURTEEN

FEBRUARY 1863

Sometimes it was so lovely here, with the river edged in ice and the soft contours of the snow-draped rocks and trees. And on those rare, cloudless days when the sun reflected off the river and slender shafts of golden light penetrated the forest canopy, glistening on the snow like something sacred, the beauty almost brought tears to Helstone's eyes. It was not often, though, that he was able to appreciate it. More often than not, he thought that he would be better off dead. All he had to do was put the rifle to his head, pull the trigger and if it fired that would be the end of his miserable existence. Oh, he had put it there all right, more than a few times, his hand trembling and scarcely able to feel the trigger, but he could never finish the job. He wanted Catherine and the children to know, in the event that his remains were found, that he had tried his best to come back to them.

Never had he ever felt such a desperate need for human company. Sometimes he cried because of his loneliness, even screamed, the sound falling dead in the forest. But lately his voice had become as coarse as a raven's and he couldn't scream anymore. So he cried, dry heaving sobs that wracked his wasting body.

When he thought back to life in the camp, his only regret was that he had not killed Rennie with the first thrust of the knife. But he had panicked when it had failed to do the job and could not help himself, fearing Rennie had much more strength than he. Later, he had counted the knife holes in Rennie's jacket and there were 10 of them. He could not remember stabbing him more than two or three times.

Rennie was always the thorn in his side, the one whose attitude irked him, the one who resented every word he spoke from his heart and every redemptive offering. "For God's sake, John," he would say. "You're driving me mad with all that drivel. Your Bible is not my Bible, so do me a favour and keep your thoughts to yourself."

It was an unforgivable affront. He could not understand why he always seemed to grate on the younger man's nerves, but it had been that way since they left London. With each passing day, he and Rennie became more antagonistic toward one another until few friendly words passed between them. He could hardly bear to look at Rennie anymore. When his pointed beard had grown down onto his chest, it reminded Helstone of the Devil himself.

Wright, on the other hand, eventually came around. Indeed, he usually got caught up in Helstone's sermons and their relationship had taken on overtones of a master and pupil. Wright would even ask him to repeat passages so that he might understand them better. It pleased Helstone that his nephew seemed to really listen and benefit from his words but beyond that, he did not see him as someone with much substance.

As the weeks passed and hopes of rescue diminished, a perpetual darkness of the soul descended upon the camp. He decided that if he was going to survive, there was only one way to do it. But when this plan of action came to him, it brought with it concern that

Rennie had had the same idea and intended to kill him. That was when he decided he should act first. He had no idea how Wright would respond or if he was even capable of responding. Of the three of them, his nephew was in the worst shape, and spent much of his time immobile, wrapped in a buffalo robe, arising only to relieve himself. Helstone did not think it likely that Wright could help Rennie even if he wanted to. With his mind made up then, it was simply a case of waiting for the night to come. That was when Rennie would be at his most vulnerable.

He recalled the events of that night with vivid clarity. He could still hear the river murmuring in the black night, and he remembered that there was a breeze in the treetops. It was funny, because sometimes those sounds were so constant that he never heard them, but on that night they were stark reminders of exactly where he was and seemed bent on driving him mad.

A part of him felt that he ought to be ashamed of himself, that he was planning to kill another human being, yet he was not. There was no shame in this savage wilderness; there was only survival. Besides, he was not doing this for selfish reasons. This was more than self-preservation: He had other people besides himself to think of, loved ones awaiting reunion.

He had to be certain Rennie was asleep before he attacked so that there was no hope of retaliation. He waited impatiently, listening for the soft snoring that would tell him the young man had fallen asleep, but it never came. Eventually, the constant exhaustion that plagued him overcame his will to stay awake and he fell asleep himself. He awakened in a sweat, feeling nauseous from a horrible nightmare of being hunted by some hellish monster. He heard both Rennie and Wright snoring yet knew instantly that something was different, that their small world had changed. The obsidian darkness inside the shelter made him think for an instant that he had been struck blind. Then the horrible realization had come rushing in on him, as swift as a striking serpent: the fire had gone out.

It had to happen eventually, but why on this night when he needed its dim light? He had no idea what time it was but was determined to stay awake until dawn. If Rennie still slept then, he would sleep forever.

The long night tried his patience. He arose once to relieve himself, stumbling in the darkness and cursing the loss of the fire. Rennie coughed, obviously awake. It was a long time before the young man finally settled down and seemed to fall back to sleep.

As the thin light of dawn crept slowly into the shelter, he felt more alive than he had for some time. Rennie was on the far side of Wright, who was in the middle lying on his back and seemingly asleep too. The time had come; it was now or never. He planned to lunge across Wright and plunge the knife deep into Rennie's heart, so it would be over quickly. He was just about to slide the weapon from its sheath and slip from beneath the buffalo robe when Rennie came hurtling at him, diving over Wright, a knife clutched in his hand.

Wright, that young man of little substance, had been awake and somehow found the strength to knock Rennie off balance. Rennie fell, sprawling over both men, down around Helstone's ankles. Grabbing his bowie, Helstone kicked out from underneath Rennie and flew at him, just as the younger man tried to rise to his knees. He landed on Rennie's back, knocking him flat, the force of the impact expelling the air from his lungs in a loud grunt. He pushed Rennie's face into the ground and thrust at him with the Bowie. The young man struggled madly. Twice, the knife hit bone and did not go in very deep. Seized by panic, Helstone stabbed Rennie again and again, until the knife finally sank to its hilt. Rennie's struggling had ceased after the first couple of blows. Blood bubbled from his mouth, along with an eerie sigh that was the sound of life leaving him.

There was blood everywhere, spattered all over Helstone's hands, arms and face, and he was panting from his exertions. When he realized at last that Rennie was dead, he collapsed on top of him, gasping for breath. Wright looked on in stunned silence, nodding his head as if assuring his uncle that he had done the right thing.

Once he had collected himself, Helstone ordered his nephew out of the way. He had to get the body outside. On his knees, he got between Rennie's legs and, wrapping his arms around them, began pulling the corpse toward the door. But he was soon drained by the effort. He could not accomplish the task by himself and turned to Wright for assistance.

"You will help, John," he ordered. "I can't do this alone. If you want food, then you will help."

Wright, who was in a state of shock, and weak, responded slowly, but between them the two men managed to pull Rennie out of the shelter. Their movements were awkward, and the gruesome task took all the strength they could muster. But Helstone had become mad with hunger and barely paused before he crawled back in the shelter to get his knife. Then, as Wright watched dumbly, he slit Rennie open from his gut to his chest cavity. "It's no different," he had croaked, "than dressing a deer."

For a while, Helstone grew stronger by the day, and so did Wright, once he made up his mind to eat. His nephew watched, a blank look on his face, as Helstone took the liver and sliced it into smaller pieces. He stuffed some in his mouth, but Wright did not ask for any for himself. Helstone slid his knife under a couple of pieces and held out the offering. "Go ahead," he urged his nephew. "The body is but a shell to house the soul and it was the soul that made it human. Now it's no different from any other animal meat." Wright took the offering in the palm of his cupped hands and stared at it for several moments, before raising it to his mouth and devouring it. There was such an air of sadness about him that Helstone had to look away.

Helstone ate slowly, savouring each piece, while Wright gorged himself. Later, when cramps had his nephew doubled up and moaning, Helstone refused to console him, lecturing him instead on gluttony.

Afterward, Wright told him that the toughest thing he had done in his life was distance himself from the chilling fact that the meat he held in his hand was part of his friend. He had thought about having to eat human flesh many times, ever since the telling of the Donner story, and had harboured doubts that he was capable of committing such a deplorable act. Starvation, however, had reshaped his thinking until he decided that he could actually eat human flesh without any qualms. The reality of it, though, was something else again. It was not so much the initial revulsion that he felt; it was the thought that he would go straight to Hell for the deed. He also said that worst thing that could have happened during those first few bites was to have someone hold up a mirror so that he could see what he was doing. It might have been far too much to bear. Wright also fretted about having to explain their actions to Mrs. Rennie and to Will and Gilbert if they were still alive, but Helstone had cut him short.

"They will understand," he said, "that it was God's will. I will make them understand. Besides, look at yourself, Johnny. You're sitting up for the first time in a long while. Your tic is gone, too."

Wright's tic had indeed gone, flown off somewhere with his youth.

The dark mood that had permeated the camp like river fog had lifted somewhat with the food, and hopes of rescue were once more entertained. Naturally, the lack of a fire was a great concern, not only for the warmth it had given but also for the light it had cast. Without it, most nights were fearsomely black. And what a blessing it had been to feel its life-giving heat radiate out onto their hands and faces, onto their backs, too, if they chose to turn away from it. Even watching its endless patterns and listening to it crackle and snap had brought no small degree of pleasure. But that luxury was gone and they spent their days wrapped in their buffalo robes.

Yet their misery was tempered somewhat by the availability of food, which provided a warmth of its own. They gorged themselves the first day, but afterward Helstone insisted that they ration the remainder of the meat. He determined the size of the portions and the number they would eat each day and, as they cleaned off a bone, it was to be added to a neat pile already begun in the corner of the shelter. If a man did not insist on some kind of order, even in the direst of circumstances, then what kind of person was he? Besides, the bones might come in handy one day if, by some miracle, a fire could be started. Boiled, they would provide a nourishing broth.

The rationing schedule only worked for a little while and was eventually ignored. He never seemed able to alleviate or control his hunger, so the size of the larder diminished proportionately. On the day they were eating the last of it, a part of Rennie's thigh, ripping the flesh from the bone like animals, the two men received the shock of their lives. Two Indians stumbled across the camp and startled the wits out of them.

Helstone had been so intent on consuming his meat that he had not heard them approach. He just happened to look up and there they were, savages dressed in animal-skin clothing, not more than 8 or 10 yards away, mouths agape, as surprised as he was. He sensed instinctively that these visitors were not their saviours, that they were the enemy, so it had only taken him a second or two to react. He grabbed his rifle and waved it at them. He did not shoot, for fear the gun would misfire and prompt them to attack. Nevertheless, his motions were a sign language that they clearly understood, and they hurried away to the north. He took the spyglass, limped out to the river, and watched them until they had disappeared from view. It did not look as if they were coming back.

Wright was so flabbergasted by the encounter that he was unable to speak for a while. When he regained his voice, he wondered aloud if scaring the Indians off had been the right thing to do. "Maybe they would have offered us help, Uncle," he suggested. But Helstone had scoffed at such a ridiculous notion. As far as he was concerned, it was only his quick thinking that had saved them from being eaten by the savages. He had come too far, at too great an expense, to die at the hands of a couple of red demons who happened to be passing by. "We will have to be more vigilant," he told Wright, but after a couple of days, they did not worry about the possibility of the Indians returning.

When the last of the food was gone, Wright began to grow weak again. His face took on a pallor that reminded Helstone of the ashes in the long-dead fire. One night in the inky darkness of the shelter the younger man said, "Uncle, I'm not going to make it … " His voice trailed off for a moment, and then he added, half whispering, "'He who eats my flesh and drinks my blood abides in me and I in him.' I will abide in you, Uncle. I want you to know that it's all right by me."

"You are not Christ, Johnny," Helstone said angrily. The audacity of the attribution had heated his blood until he caught

Wright's meaning. It was just his way of offering himself as food; giving his approval, in other words. He suddenly saw his nephew in a different light. When added to the way he had pushed Rennie away during the night of the attack, Helstone began to think that perhaps there was more substance to the young man than he had given him credit for.

"I won't do it for myself, Johnny," he said. "You know that. It'll be for Catherine and the boys. They need me home." His voice cracked with this last sentiment.

Wright choked back a sob but said nothing else. Helstone fleetingly wondered if his nephew had been thinking about Elizabeth and the girls, that perhaps he was needed by them just as much. Probably not. Wright no longer looked at the photograph of Elizabeth that he had brought on the journey, and some time ago had asked his uncle to put it in his Bible for safekeeping. Besides which, he really had no other family left. His mother, Helstone's older sister, with whom Helstone never had much of a relationship, had died a decade ago from consumption, and his drunkard father had deserted them years before that. Insofar as Elizabeth was concerned, she was a shrew who would no doubt ensure that his children soon forgot him. Anyway, none of it mattered. All that mattered was that Wright willingly offered himself for sustenance. It was the right thing to do and the sooner it came to pass the better. Helstone began to will his nephew to die.

The next night Wright began to breathe strangely, like a rasp pulled across a board, and there did not seem to be any pattern to it. Helstone expected him to die during the night, but by dawn the worst of the crisis had passed and Wright's breathing grew easier. Several times, he called for Elizabeth. A wave of disappointment rose in Helstone like bile and made him furious.

Damn him to Hell, anyway, he thought. Why won't he die, so that I can eat? It was unkind of him to promise himself and then hang onto life so obstinately.

Another long night passed. Wright muttered longings for Elizabeth and his breathing was laboured, and with every breath the hunger inside Helstone seemed to grow tenfold. Anger reared in him, too, and climbed to nearly uncontrollable levels. Finally, he could not hold back any longer. When Wright was still breathing the next morning, he crawled to where a small axe was leaning against the wall of the shelter. He reasoned that it would be quicker than the knife. He picked it up and walked on his knees back to his nephew. Raising the axe in the air, he swung it down on the young man's head, but his aim was off and the dull blade only struck a glancing blow. He saw Wright's eyes open wide and then, just as he had done with Rennie, he panicked at the ridiculous assumption that somehow Wright would rise up and slay him. He struck harder and more accurately, until there was so much blood he knew that his nephew had to be dead. He did not bother to pull the corpse outside and took the liver straight away. The strength it gave him seemed almost superhuman.

That was how long ago? He did not know. Only that he was alone and had been for some time. No. Alone was not quite the appropriate word. It smacked too much of a temporary condition, that one would sooner or later be joined by other people, whereas in his case, such an event was not even a remote possibility. And God, though he spoke to Him often, was not answering anymore. He was *abandoned,* left to rot in this wilderness prison, this frozen Hell, his body to become fodder for animals, his possessions booty for savages. He could not imagine a more pathetic ending to his life.

During those moments when he wanted more than anything to live, there was no end to his worries. His hands and feet, for example, had worsened since the loss of the fire and at times were unbearably painful. His limbs did not always respond to his will and sometimes his entire body felt numb. Then for no explainable reason he would feel comparatively good, able to hold his food in his hands and move around with relative ease. But he knew that he would eventually lose the use of his limbs altogether, that it was simply a matter of time.

He worried about his bodily functions. He did not know how long it had been since he had last defecated, only that ages had passed and that his steady diet of meat was likely the cause. His bowels felt as if they were being wrung the same way that Catherine wrung the clothes after a wash. He strained to move them until he thought he might burst, but to no avail. He became so desperate that he whittled a smooth stick to insert into his rectum to try to pry his stool out but had not the dexterity to perform the task. To think that he had left a perfectly comfortable home and travelled 2,000 miles for this! Sometimes when he thought about it, the irony made him want to weep.

He brooded over his relationship with God, or seeming lack of it now, and wondered if the journey that he and his companions had set out on so long ago might have had a more favourable outcome if he had done just one thing differently. He wracked his brain to figure out what that might be but came up with nothing. He had his faults, no doubt about that, but other than the occasional blasphemy and the ribald stories he loved to tell in male company, he was no great sinner. True, he had planned Rennie's death, but had actually killed him in self-defence, and Johnny ... well, hadn't his nephew offered himself for sustenance? He had only eaten their flesh because he wanted to live. Was that such a sin? Perhaps so, for God had become strangely silent lately and that was cause for great concern. Just yesterday, he had hobbled out to the riverbank in the twilight to look at the sky. He did not go there much anymore because from that vantage point, the world was too big and his place in it too insignificant. The shelter was a more manageable space. But he had needed a glimpse of the heavens because that was where God resided. The sun had shone most of the day, but it was down behind the mountains and a shaving of moon was rising in the east. Ice had quieted the river to a whisper. He lifted his face heavenward. "Why do you give succour to some and ignore others? Why do you ignore me? Talk to me!" he screamed, not knowing if the words had come out of his mouth or if they were just inside his head. "Talk to me!" But he was crushed by an avalanche of silence.

He frequently lapsed into daydreams, not only of the God who had forsaken him, but also of Catherine and the children. How old were the boys now? Had they grown up? Such thoughts confused him, especially at those times when he thought he had been here for years. Perhaps his children had children of their own now and he was a grandfather. The thought both warmed his heart and caused him great despair, for it was not likely that he would ever see any of his family again.

Insofar as the weather was concerned, it had been a terrible winter overall. Many storms had passed over the area and the days were mostly dull and always sub-zero. The river looked frozen now, hard enough to walk on, but he didn't have the strength. Recently though, there had been a spell of good weather, when the sun shone and softened the snow and turned the surface of the ice on the river slushy. It almost made a man appreciate just being alive, even in his condition. Then the worst blizzard of the season roared in and the wind keened like a grieving widow for two days, blowing trees down along the river and sending branches crashing to the forest floor. When at last it stopped, the silence throbbed in his ears like a demonic drum.

It was on such a day that someone approached the camp. He heard voices and his heart leapt into his throat. Had they come to rescue him at last? Had Will and Gilbert known that he, above everyone else, had the will to survive for so long a time? No. Sounds of a rescue party would have come from the south. These came from the north. At first, he could not discern what the voices were saying, and when the shapes of the words finally came to him, he could not understand them for they were not English. They belonged to a language he did not recognize. Then the fog in his brain cleared. They were Indian words. Indian! In his terror, he forgot about his sore hands and feet, grabbed the rifle that he kept near him at all times, and scrambled to get up. He waited, holding on to the shelter with his free hand so that he would not fall, swaying slightly from dizziness. If the savages had come for the spoils of the camp, thinking all of its occupants were dead, they were in for a mighty big surprise. He would give them no warning this time. He loaded the gun, put the first Indian in his sights and pulled the trigger.

'Kwah raised his hand to signal those behind him to stop. They had reached the entrance to the long rapid and would now have to proceed with caution. Somewhere along this stretch of the river was the camp of the eaters of human flesh. 'Kwah and his cousins, Taya and Tsohtaih, had come from their village on the lake beyond the lake from which the river flows north, with a single purpose: to kill them.

They had moved swiftly, despite the inclement weather, for they were Déné and the Déné believed that once a man tastes the flesh of humans, he will want more and has to be stopped. It had happened among his people and the fact that these cannibals were white men made no difference. They would also have to be stopped.

He had had occasion to deal with white men before, trading furs at the fort to the south of here, and found many of them unscrupulous and greedy. They were also tough to negotiate with, especially the fort's chief whom 'Kwah considered ruthless. Nevertheless, it was common knowledge that white men usually had in their possession many useful items, not the least of which were rifles. That this was true of the flesh-eaters was told to him by those who first passed the camp and saw it with their own eyes. This journey, then, would serve two purposes: It would rid the world of men not fit to live and increase 'Kwah's and his cousins' wealth, making a trek not normally done during the harsh winter months well worth the effort.

They came upon a straight stretch of beach, lined with a neat row of tall cottonwoods edging the river and fronting the spruce forest. This was the spot where their informants had said the campsite was located. Taya and Tsohtaih had been talking, and he motioned them to be quiet. 'Kwah kept his eyes peeled for any sign of human disturbance and sniffed the air. There was an odour about white men, not entirely offensive, that required some getting used to. Given the right wind conditions, he could smell them several yards off. So far, there was only the smell of river and forest.

He sensed the movement before he saw it, but his keen eyes moved directly toward it: a wild man, one of the eaters of the dead, with unruly hair, scraggly beard and tattered clothes. And with a gun pointed at them. 'Kwah and his cousins dove for cover.

He was surprised that he did not hear a gunshot. He heard instead a desperate cry, then the sound of someone crashing through the forest, and guessed that the gun had jammed and the man was now trying to flee. 'Kwah peeked carefully from his cover. He saw the back of the man moving among the trees. There appeared to be no one else about. He pulled a hatchet from a leather loop around his waist and he and his cousins took off in pursuit.

Afterword

John Giscombe, the black trapper whose name has been given to the rapids beside the camp, was the man who discovered the grisly remains, the details of which were reported in the *British Colonist* on December 14, 1863. Giscome told how William and Gilbert Rennie had come to his cabin on the same day that four Indians had arrived. He said that two of the four Indians, after stating they would not do it, actually did go up to the rapids where they found the camp. There, they witnessed two men eating a third, "all but his legs which they held in their hands … and were tearing the raw flesh from the bones." The Indians told Giscome that they had only wanted to light a fire for the stranded men who threatened them with guns. At a later date, the Indians told him of the attack on the camp and the slaying of the last survivor. With this news, Thomas Charles had asked him, since he was heading up that way on a prospecting trip, to examine the camp himself.

He found it about 50 miles above Fort George. The canoe was still lying close by, but the Indians had carried off everything else worth removing. "Inside the camp, in one corner, there lay a small pile of bones, carefully packed together. Among them was the skull of a young man with the whole of the lower jaw and a row of good teeth still perfect. He [Giscome] also found the skull of another man, which had eight prints of an axe upon it where it had evidently been chopped open. Some of the bones were still bloody and were half chewed at the ends."

Beyond the camp, he found a patch of hair, still attached to a piece of skin. He could not find the third man, so he "collected the bones, dug a grave and buried them, leaving a written notice in case the spot should be visited by other persons." His Indian guides presumed that "he was writing to say that they had murdered the last man. Giscome appeased them when one of their number said that he knew where the third man could be found. He was lying 300 to 400 yards from the camp, over a rise, stripped of his clothes and several cuts from a hatchet on his head and body."

At an Indian camp farther north, Giscome saw a "small Bible with the photograph of a young lady in it, but no name to indicate which of the party it belonged to. He also saw two axes, a spyglass and some utensils, which the Indians said they had removed from the camp, but they would not disclose everything with reference to the murder of the survivor. They further said that the blankets, carpet sacks and pocketbooks belonging to the deceased were in the possession of some Indians about four days travel from there and that they intended taking them to Mr. Charles." It is not known whether they did so.

Among other things shown to Giscome by the Indians was "young Rennie's coat with several knife holes in the back of it. They said they had found it just as it was in the camp."

From the statements of the Indians and his personal inspection, Giscome could only conclude that "the poor men had been reduced by starvation and cold to the last extremities, and had actually killed and eaten one another. They must have existed for about 10 weeks, the longest liver having to all appearances suffered a cruel death at the hands of the Indians for the sake of plunder."

History does not record what Gilbert Rennie did for the remainder of his life. It does show, however, that Will returned to Williams Creek, alone, and for reasons known only to him. Perhaps he needed to lay some ghosts to rest. Whatever sent him there, the days of the big strikes were over, but he had prudently packed his shoemaker's tools and opened a shop in Barkerville. There was no shortage of work in a community where a man at the bottom of a mine needed only a few days to ruin a good pair of boots and where there was no shortage of money to replace them. As his wallet fattened, he invested in a couple of mines that must have paid dividends, for the record shows that he hobnobbed with the wealthier citizens of Barkerville. Attending soirees in tiny gold-camp houses did not quite have the status of attending one at Eldon House, but it may very well have been a satisfying substitute.

He joined the Masons and along the way met and fraternized with some of the stars of the gold rush, those who left their indelible stamp on the event and on history. To name but a few: Billy Barker, the first man to strike it rich, whose name would be given to the town; Robert Stevenson who, with John Cameron, made the biggest strike ever on the creek and helped him fulfill his promise to take his dead wife home; John Bowron, one of the original Overlanders who came west with the McMicking party, opened Barkerville's first library and later had a chain of lakes named after him; and Wellington Delaney Moses, the town's black barber whose shop exists to this day. It would not be unreasonable to speculate that he probably knew Madam Fanny Bendixon as well, not to mention some of the young ladies in her employ.

On August 29, 1880, he married a widow named Catherine Evans, whose husband had been a member of the infant British

Columbia Legislature. Will was 48 and she was 10 years his junior. The newlyweds left Barkerville, their destination unknown, and here history thumbs its nose at whatever desires we might have to know what became of them.

But two pictures of William Rennie remain, both taken in Barkerville. One is a group photo of him and his fellow Masons. Taken from a distance, it speaks little of the man who knew such tragedy and such sorrow. But the other picture is telling. It is a formal portrait. He stands with his right arm resting on a plinth upon which sits a vase of flowers. The backdrop is a wall, half-wainscotted and half-canvas. He wears an odd-looking suit, almost like coveralls, that is double breasted, with a belt pulled uncomfortably tight around his waist. He has on a bow tie that lies askew across a white shirt. A hat tilts back above a high forehead. His boots are shiny and appear new, as if he made them specifically for the photograph. He looks directly into the camera with a hard, almost defiant glare, as if to say, "You can't know me." But if a photograph mirrors the soul, then the soul of this man is bared for all to see.

If one looks closely at his narrow and wispily bearded face, even without the knowledge of his past, it is easy to see beyond the hardness, beyond the defiance. If one looks *with* such knowledge, the veneer crumbles into dust. There is fear in those eyes, on that face: fear that the world will learn things about him that he would rather it did not know. There is bitterness too, a heart-rending bitterness about things that ordinary mortals without his experience could not possibly comprehend. But most of all there is anger, directed at himself, perhaps, and a world where Fate jabs randomly at the human race, landing a bruising blow here and a fatal one there. And God help the poor soul who happens to be in the way.